DEATH & NIGHTINGALES

Eugene McCabe was born in Glasgow in 1930. His work includes *Heritage and Other Stories* and *Victims*, a short novel which won the Holtby Award from the Royal Society of Literature (1976). Eugene McCabe has also written a number of plays.

ALSO BY EUGENE McCABE

Stage Plays

King of the Castle
Breakdown
Pull Down a Horseman
Swift
Gale Day

Television plays adapted from original prose works

A Matter of Conscience
Some Women on the Island
The Funeral
Cancer
Heritage
Siege
Roma
Music at Annahullion

Prose

Victims
Heritage and Other Stories
Cyril
Christ in the Field.

Eugene McCabe

DEATH &
NIGHTINGALES

V

VINTAGE

Published by Vintage 1998

5 8 10 9 7 5

Copyright © Eugene McCabe 1992

The right of Eugene McCabe to be identified as the author of this work
has been asserted by him in accordance with the Copyright, Designs and
Patents Act, 1988

I am grateful to the Clogher Historical Society, and its editor, Theo
McMahon, for permission to refer to the diary of James Donnelly,
Bishop of Clogher, 1865 to 1893, edited by Patrick Mulligan, late
Bishop of Clogher, 1970 to 1979. For images and details of eighteenth-
century fur-trading in Canada I am also indebted to Peter C. Newman's
history *Company of Adventurers*. I am aware that aficionados of Percy
French will know that he was closer to thirty than fifty in the year 1883.

First published in Great Britain by
Martin Secker & Warburg Ltd 1992

Vintage
Random House, 20 Vauxhall Bridge Road, London SW1V 2SA

Random House Australia (Pty) Limited
20 Alfred Street, Milsons Point, Sydney
New South Wales 2061, Australia

Random House New Zealand Limited
18 Poland Road, Glenfield
Auckland 10, New Zealand

Random House (Pty) Limited
Endulini, 5a Jubilee Road, Parktown 2193, South Africa

The Random House Group Limited Reg. No. 954009
www.randomhouse.co.uk

A CIP catalogue record for this book
is available from the British Library

ISBN 0 7493 9868 X

Papers used by Random House are natural, recyclable
products made from wood grown in sustainable forests. The
manufacturing processes conform to the environmental
regulations of the country of origin.

Printed and bound in Norway by
AIT Trondheim AS

For J. C. who gave me
the bones of this tale
in an April garden

All is oblique
There's nothing level in our cursed natures
But direct villainy.

Timon of Athens
Act 4, scene 3

I

A lack of bird-call, a sense of encroaching light and then far away the awful dawn bawling of a beast in great pain. For a while it stopped, as though birds and ditch creatures were listening, respectful of approaching death. Then she heard the beating of her heart and saw herself in Billy's study reading about medieval medicine from *The Chemist and Druggist 1880*. 'A cure for insomnia: the milk of a human female placed on the forehead will induce sleep. Place the heart of a nightingale under the patient's pillow. Poisons: aconite, arsenic, ergot, oil of bitter almonds. The Reverend J. H. Timmins, vicar of West Malling, was acquitted on the 18th of July of a charge of manslaughter. Defendant believed the teaspoon of oil of bitter almonds administered to his wife was oil of sweet almonds.'

In the dark pantry off the scullery she was looking into the hanging press full of veterinary medicines and gadgetry, and yes, there it was, a small, pale yellow bottle labelled 'oil of bitter almonds' with a separate label which said: 'POISON'. She put it to her nose and sniffed. The astringency of death invaded her lungs. As she watched herself pouring out a teaspoon for Billy's protruding tongue her whole body began to shake. The teaspoon trembled, spilling, and she awoke to the bawling of a beast reverberating round the stillness of her bedroom. Then a dark silence.

She sat up startled, staring out into quarter-light, into the blackness of beech branches. The agonised bawling was now unmistakable and pitiful; and there it was again: blaring, blaring, blaring. From where? The house-field? Beyond? some beast jostled down the ravine hanging by a leg or neck? A calving cow in trouble? or common bloat from gorging on the flush of May grass? Silence for thirty seconds and then a sudden mutter from Billy's room.

She was up at the window, dressing, when it started again. She went out to the hall, tapped softly on Billy Winters' door and went in. She was aware of a lingering hum of malt whiskey and cigar smoke, a familiar body smell mixed with the sweet odour of clematis coming through the open bay-window that had permeated the upper hall and bedrooms since late April. He was sprawled uncovered on a carved bed in a grey night-shirt, his mouth open. The bawling now seemed more pronounced through his window. She touched his arm, nudging him a second time as she said 'Sir'. For an instant his eyelids half opened; closed. He turned away. If she forced him to wake and listen to the beast he would be agitated into shirt and trousers and go stumbling down the rough avenue to the gatelodge for Jim Ruttledge and help. Heart seizure? How simple if he was dead buried and gone. What then? Do I want any of this? The heartbreak of this place? Love it and hate it like no place else on earth, tomorrow I leave it forever.

She stood looking at the back of his head, aware that she was scarcely a reach away from his clothes on the chair, the gold chain clinched through a belt loop and, at the end of it, the keys to the quarry strong-room, the roll-top desk in the study, and the massive safe behind the panelling in the dining-room.

The bawling started again as she left his room, went out to the landing and down to the turn of the staircase. A door off the stairs led to a narrow corridor and a small return room over the kitchen where Mercy Boyle slept under a skylight with oleographs of the Sacred Heart and Parnell. Long after midnight Beth had heard her coming in from a love meeting or a crossroads dance. Heartless now to waken and involve her. That left Mickey Dolphin and Mercy's brother Gerry asleep in a loft across the yard. Mickey would be hungover, Gerry nervous and excitable. She would manage better without them.

She went on down past the big etching of the Boyne battle, the cow pastoral and the lake scene, into the grey glimmer from the fanlight in the lower hall; past the black furniture and on through to the kitchen and scullery.

From a drawer of the hanging veterinary press she took the canula, a hollow pointed instrument with a clearing plunger, and put it in the pocket of her skirt. Closing the press she saw again the bottle marked 'oil of bitter almonds'. She closed the press, pulled on her field boots, crossed the cobbled yard and went out – under the arched entry and down the back lane. Under rearing beech cradling a few dying stars, she felt a sense of light and openness as she left the lane for the haggard field: a white owl flitting in a group of lime trees, the scut of a rabbit's tail bouncing as it made for the safety of a ditch. She passed through the limes, emerging from their cathedral dark to a gate which led to the fountain hill. At the top of this field there was a ring-fort encircled by pines growing on a high bank. She began to climb. She could see the black conifer shapes against the redness of the coming day. She was certain the bawling had come from the fort or near it.

She went through a gap in the bank. Inside there was a grouping of cows, agitated and lowing towards a blue shorthorn cow on her side, her whitish belly ballooned out, eyes rolling, her head banging against the ground.

'Poor beast, poor beast,' Beth muttered, 'I'm coming,' and went over to her. Recognising her, the cow lowed quietly and kept still. 'You'll be all right,' Beth said, as much to give herself confidence as to lessen the beast's fear. She had seen Jim Ruttledge use the canula once. He seemed to drive it down with great force inches from the hinch bone.

She breathed deeply until her hands steadied and then thrust with sudden sharpness. The point pierced through to the cow's stomach: the trapped gas hissing out like a wet log on a hot fire, a rush of foul air mixed with tiny bubbles of blood. She stood by with the plunger in case the small opening of the canula blocked; her hand over her mouth and nose, half-gagging, trying not to breathe. The smell became so pervasive and foul that she moved away, aware that her legs felt rubbery, her stomach queasy. In less than two minutes the distended balloon had slackened, the loud hiss slowing to a faint air release; then silence.

Five minutes later the blue cow sat up naturally, blinking very slowly, shaking her head. The circle of heads watched until she uttered feebly. All then responded as she stood, her feet spread for a minute, before beginning a slow wavering walk towards a gap out of the fort. Watching this, Beth became aware of birds again: a solitary crane, crows, and daws, raucous and

4

flapping, a chorus of starlings wheeling, whirling high above, small birds ruffling and chirruping in the greening thorns, celebratory.

She left the hollow of the fort by the north gap that looked down the long field to the Lower Lough. She could just make out Corvey Island, part of her mother's dowry, the other part a shorthorn bull calf. She had once heard Billy mutter to himself 'a scrub bull and a scrub island!' In fact the bull had grown to be a wonder and Corvey Island was beautiful. On the map it was fish-shaped and she knew there were wild goats on it. Once as a child she had asked:

'Is it true Mama? can I live there by myself?'

'If you want.'

'Forever and ever?'

'Would you be happy?'

'It's the nicest place in the whole world.'

'What would you do there all by yourself?'

'Well . . . I'd tame a wild goat and milk it . . . I'd catch fish.'

'Yes?'

'I'd learn to make butter.'

'That's good.'

'And I'd pick blackberries.'

'Yes?'

'And I'd have apple trees . . . I'd be happy.'

'Would visitors be allowed?'

'Yes but no fighting on my island or crying or shouting at night.'

And she remembered that both Billy and her mother were so startled by her directness that she said immediately: 'I was just joking.'

* * *

The mist had cleared across the lough. She could see the island now, the brightening countryside on the far shore: Tirkennedy where her mother came from. I must fix it now in memory she thought because not for years, probably never again would she see what one day she imagined could be paradise. Tomorrow at dawn she would be in the railyard at Enniskillen looking for the guard's-wagon of a goods train bound for Belfast. From there she would take a cab to a hotel on Royal Avenue; that night she would board a packet steamer for Glasgow. Then a train to London where she would write to Liam telling him of her whereabouts. He would join her there and they would begin their lives together.

As the house and beech trees around it came into view it seemed to her more real than anything she had planned with Liam Ward. She felt herself swallowing hard against a sudden pang of nausea. Fear? The life now growing within? A sudden cracked barking came from the top of a stone staircase leading to a loft. 'Don't be silly, Bran, you know well who I am!' The old labrador got up and came stiffly and heavily down the stone staircase: 'Don't you?'

The wall-clock in the kitchen told her it was a quarter to six. She opened the firebox of the big leaded Denver stove where a heavy beech log still smouldered from the night before. From the floor of the oven she took out small tinder-dry twigs and laid them crossways in the firebox, topped it up with turf, closed off the draught and placed a heavy black kettle on top. She turned and climbed the staircase to the upper hall.

The sun had partially come through mist and cloud into her bedroom opposite Billy Winters'. She stood for a while listening to him breathe, and then went in and laid dressed on her unmade bed. She could feel blood pulsing

6

under her eyelids. She covered her eyes with the palms of her hands, trying not to think forward. That was too frightening. Back?

What she remembered seemed mostly to be shouting from behind closed doors, passionate screaming from window to yard, things broken, thumped, thrown and torn, the dread of being near while such frenzies broke as they seemed to so simply, so often . . . Her mother talking in the dining-room about Tirkennedy, where she was born: an eighty-acre tenancy across the lough, part of the Corry estate, 'old Irish, real gentry' she insisted, where her father, 'Red' Jack Maguire, was a horse-buyer-cum-horse-trainer; he was the best in Ulster and maybe in Ireland. He had married her grandmother, Rosina Quinn, a parlour-maid in the Corry house, and they had three children – of which she, Catherine, was the youngest. She then described how she had met Billy Winters at the R.D.S. in 1860 where her pacer 'Pride of Erne' had not only eclipsed but outclassed (and she had accented the word 'outclassed') all other entries; how he had plagued her to marry him, 'I was an old woman of twenty-nine, he was a child of twenty-three'; the wedding arrangements in Corry's private chapel; special dispensation from Armagh and how a Belfast or Dublin journal had described Billy as 'one of Ulster's foremost young businessmen' and her mother as having 'the white skin and flaming hair of an older, more romantic Ireland'. During the telling of this Billy Winters had kept silent. When she had finished he said:

'You left out the best part Cathy!'

Her mother stared back uncertainly as Billy went on:

'Remember? when your father came out of the closet his trousers round his ankles and tumbled down

7

that staircase into the hall: drunk, in the middle of all the guests, all laughing because Jimmy Donnelly who married us had gone on and on and on in a very long wedding speech about the ancientness and Irishness and the grandeur of the name Maguire ... because Winters don't you know is a nothing name, and here he was, father of the bride, the great horse trader, the Maguire chief himself, a clown with his trousers down ... as they say hereabouts, "a comical class of a comedown" ... or, if you want, a comedown for the comical class! Your brother Jimmy was too footless to help, and your Aunt Annie took a weak turn, so it was the bride and the bride's mother who rushed to make him decent ... The whole country had it the next day: quite an outing for the ancient name!'

For about a minute or longer her mother had stared out the window, a vein pulsing in her neck, the blood of temper rising like a barometer to her face. When she spoke her voice was shaky:

'When there were no fields here, before the Greenes and the Brownes, the Winters and the Somers, the rat-poor robbers with nothing names came here to rob us of what was ours, Maguire was a proud name and still is.'

'Oh the pride's there to be sure,' Billy said, 'and sweet bugger-all to prop it up!'

Then her mother had smashed a jug or bowl against the closing door as Billy left, and wept with rage before following him out to the hall, holding on to the banister as she screamed up the staircase after him:

'Why must you keep on and on at me like a bloody fishwoman?'

'Who are you to look down on fish women?'

'I look down on no one.'

8

'Some spunky boyo looked down on you once, that's for sure.'

Her mother had covered her ears and screamed 'Stop!' so loudly that Beth backed away from the dining-room door, covering her own ears. When she uncovered them she heard:

'I have begged your forgiveness for one mistake.'

'"Mistake" is a nice word!'

'What word do you prefer?'

Then Billy's voice biting out in bitter response:

'Miscegenation, misbegotten; Rome's cup of poison in your belly when we married! That child's not kin to me and won't inherit, do you hear me, won't inherit; she nor her kind will ever cut my trees, burn my turf, pluck my apples, milk my cows, quarry my stone, and never plough my acres . . . ever!'

'Jesus! You're like a craw-sick parrot! . . . my, my, my, my, my. You stole it from us and you know you stole it.'

Later that night her mother came into her bed. Below they could hear Billy trying to pick out tunes on the piano. Too drunk to manage chords he attempted melodies with one finger; then it was as if he was banging with both fists on the piano, shouting. They could hear him on the staircase and then fumbling about in the bedroom across the hall. Then silence, through which she became aware that her mother was trembling:

'Why does Papa shout "belly" and things like that?'

'He's drunk.'

'Did he hit you?'

'I wish he had.'

'We should go away Mama.'

'We can't.'

9

'Why?'

'Because we can't.'

'He's a bully . . . That last time when he hit you, you said you'd kill him.'

'That was very wrong of me.'

'Well *I* hate him.'

'You don't, love.'

'I do.'

'Never talk that way, that's terrible talk and I love him mostly.'

'You don't love him, Mama: you can't!'

'I can . . . I do . . . go to sleep.'

And for years after the word 'inherit' had echoed in her head: 'not inherit, not inherit, not inherit.' At first she thought it meant a running thing like a hare: that she would never run in the fields like other children. When she found out what it meant it seemed worse: 'to cast out, to cast off, to disown, to reject, to disallow; to be disowned by a father; to lose everything.' At her mother's graveside she had lost everything. Rain and the yellow clay and the coffin being lowered into water flooding up. Billy's disinheriting arm round her shoulder and the sobbing, the end of everything. Weeks of grieving and praying that death would end it all. Away then to a convent in Monaghan. Christmas and Easter with Billy at Clonoula, where he seemed to have drunk and talked a lot, and sang, and sat on the side of her bed and wept; and she had wept with him. Once trying to describe the manner of her mother's death he had been unable to continue. Years later she got details from Winnie Ruttledge in the kitchen of the gatelodge: the arrival of the bull-calf from Tirkennedy as part of her mother's dowry – and how proud she was of it, telling everyone it was called Cooley, and how everyone declared it a wonder calf, its uncommon depth, length, bone and muscle, the power of its neck and shoulders, and an eye in its head no countryman would ever turn his back on.

As the years went on Cooley grew headstrong, ripping the copper ring from his nose, smashing his way through gates and gaps to neighbour farms, swimming across the lough to get to cows and heifers summering on the larger islands. They'd had to confine him in the stone house behind the cattle crush in the upper yard. One day he turned savage, went for Jim Ruttledge: 'Only Mickey Dolphin was close by I'd be a widow now, and when the boss heard tell of this he said he'll have to go.

'Next day as they were loadin' him on to a trailer the sky opened. Your mother come into the yard at that minute with her cush and gig. She could see nothing with the blind of rain. The two men had the ramp up when the bull turned in the trailer, whipping it with his head, and sent the pair of boys tumbling across the yard like two twigs. Then out with him roaring mad and he had the cush gored and the gig coped and your mother in the air tossed and ripped pitiful before Mickey caught him a lash in the eye and my man got an axe to his skull. And true as God I heard the blares and trumpets of him down here half a mile away till they got a knife across his throat. Christ in Heaven what a shambles, the whole street runnin' water and blood and every man and woman in the place hysterical; but she was dead your mother, the boss holdin' her head off the street: dead dead dead and covered with a horse blanket, all to her white lovely face. And when I took courage to lift the blanket I seen . . . merciful Jesus . . . a wee blind bairn tore from her womb and it no bigger nor a bonham.'

Brother? Sister? She placed her hands on her womb. There was nothing to feel. The 'bairn' conceived with Liam Ward would be less than kitten-sized. She would not tell him till their plan was accomplished, till they were well away from Clonoula, from Fermanagh, from Ireland. Aboard ship and looking back she would tell him, they were beginning both a new life and a new family.

'Miss Lisbeth, Beth, Miss Beth!'

Mercy Boyle's face was very close. Outside the window the brightest of white May light on the palest of green beech leaves. And far above a high clear sky.

'That's Petey Reilly at the back door, Miss.'

'Who?'

'The Canon's man . . . he's here with a message for the boss. Did you sleep all night in your clothes?'

'No, no, I'll explain when I come down, you tell the boss, Mercy.'

'I will . . . Happy birthday, Miss.'

Mercy placed a small package on the bedspread and left the room, closing the door quietly. Beth untied the green ribbon, folding back tissue paper. Inside she found an ornate brass locket. It clicked open to reveal the chiselled features and hypnotic eyes of Charles Stewart Parnell.

2

Am I awake now or asleep, or waking? Most likely
waking, yes; light. Beth's birthday. Was she in the room
just now or a while back? Girl-smell, clematis, woman-
smell, twenty-five. Birthdays; deathdays. When's mine?
Where? Bed? Aboard ship? Chair? Stable? Field? Church?
Quarry? Matters not ... but how? Slowly? Agony,
bowel-slip and terror, oh Jesus mercy, forgive, forgive,
forgive a wretched sinner, always Jesus! Suddenly on
highway or byway, at horse-fair or home-farm, William
Hudson Winters, my name in a column, table of death,
deceased. Like a shot; bang! black end, gone, no more.
Eternity ...

Here lieth all the dead Winters in the cold north
ground of the province of Ulster.

Here lieth all the women of the dead Winters in the
cold north ground of the province of Ulster.

Here lieth all the infants and children of all the dead
Winters in the cold north ground of the province of
Ulster. It awaits.

Poor Mama's silly jingle.

'I'll tell you a story bout Billy MacClory.

Will I begin it

That's all that's in it!'

Is that all? Full stop?

Or do we journey onto God's house, morning star, house of gold ... My grandfather's. Is it safe in that old safe? Is it? Who's knocking? Yes? More knocking, again. Yes! Knocking, louder:

'Yes!' Billy Winters said, jerking awake on to his elbows.

'I've a message, Sorr, and your hot water.'

'Hold on Mercy ... a message ... who from?'

'Canon McManus's man called.'

'What! hold on.'

Billy Winters bedrolled over, swinging his legs onto the square of faded Indian carpet. Thrusting his arms into a dressing-gown he padded across the pine boards to the bedroom door:

'When ... who did you say?'

'This minute, Sorr, Petey Reilly, the Canon's man. He said the Canon would call here on his way back from Mass.'

'That would be now.'

'Yes, Sorr.'

Her confessor, Canon Leo McManus. What does she tell him?

Mercy turned and went down towards the turn of the staircase. Behind her, outside the hall window and beyond, the house-field sloped north toward the high ring-fort that looked down on the lower lake.

Dear God the wonder and beauty, of light and water, of field, tree, and sky ... May, what a month to be alive and I woke up dreaming of death.

Below he could hear cow-chains and buckets and mild lowing. He called:

'Mercy.'

'Sorr?'

'Where is Miss Beth now?'

'She'll be about the kitchen or dairy.'

'You do know what day it is?'

Mercy smiled through crooked teeth.

'Me mother has a cake made special and I have something I give her.'

'You're a good girl, Mercy; I'll be down directly.'

And she was: discreet, hardworking, loyal.

Mercy had left the white enamel jug of hot water on a table in the upper hall. He carried it to the wash-stand, poured it into a basin and began preparing to shave. In the bow of a south window there was a ship's telescope alongside a tripod shaving mirror with candle holders. A north window between the wash-stand and wardrobe looked down on the yard with its two arched entrances, slated out-buildings, the garden, orchard and paddocks leading to the haggard. A rivulet of spring water from the fountain hill surfaced in the yard near the byre in a stone-faced pool. Everlasting. Never failed in drought, nor froze in the bitterest winter. Swirling now round two copper cans keeping the milk and cream sweet from churning to churning. Ancient system: glazed crocks, creak of oxen carts in streets of Jerusalem, the squares of Rome. Fountains, cisterns, springs, aquaducts, the armies of Constantine crucifying Europe for Christ, crusaders butchering in Asia, looting for Christendom.

A Christian man myself, my breed brutal as any Turk, unkind mankind, aye and womankind to bear and suckle such. My dead love Cathy, mother of Elizabeth, father unknown. 'One of two,' she taunted once . . . fountain of old sorrows . . . her birthday today.

❋   ❋   ❋

As he moved the shaving mirror for better light his blinking eye caught a movement in the yard below, a blue shorthorn cow plodding across the cobbled yard towards a stone cattle-crush followed by Jim Ruttledge. Something glinted near the cow's hip-bone as she walked into the crush . . . canula is it? Bloat?

Jim had closed a small iron gate behind the cow and was removing the canula as Billy Winters opened the window and called down:

'A touch of bloat, Jim?'

'Aye.'

Jim Ruttledge knew where Billy was. He did not look up. Well over seventy and sturdier than most men of fifty he had been working here at Clonoula before Billy Winters was born.

'Bad?'

'She'll over it.'

'You were lucky to catch her.'

'It was Miss Beth got her; heard the blaring a fair while back.'

So there *was* an animal blaring, no dream. How many women, girls, would brave into half-dark fields to ram a canula into a bloated, dying beast. Her birthday the worst day of my life. She's twenty-five today, another year. Anniversary. When is poor Mama's deathday? Blackberry time. September's end. Leaf-fall. How she played and sang long long ago when I was young, as simply as others breathe – hauntingly of love and love's dream lost forever. And to die then with such grace and humour . . . Give away this, that and the other; burn and throw away this, that and the other . . . and when you've that all done . . . throw away me.

Quietly as he shaved, Billy Winters began to hum a

Moore melody, pausing when he heard, half-way down the avenue, the faint scatter of hooves on gravel. He looked out the side of the bow-window. Yes, there he was, topper, frock-coat, astride a grey horse, carrying his silver-banded riding-crop: Canon Leo McManus in full canonicals. As Billy pulled on a collarless shirt, deferential grey trousers and a waistcoat he heard himself sing quietly:

'Rule Romania, Romania rules the taigs,
Poor Rosie's childer ever, ever, shall be slaves.'

3

For Canon Leo McManus the best part of his ministry was travelling on horseback the by-roads, farms, villages and townlands of Upper Fermanagh. On the walls of his dining-room in the parish house at Dromcoo he had land commission maps pencil-marked, and could tell at a glance the name, status and religion of the owner. He kept a separate register for emigrants, corresponding with those who had prospered and trying to persuade them to buy back, where possible, what he called in his circular 'The Escheated or stolen patrimony of our forebears'. A matter of some disappointment was that Con Cunningham of Los Angeles, and Barney Hughes of London, who could between them have bought the entire county, failed to reply. Many others did and proved helpful. The county was evenly divided between Catholic and Protestant; time and determination, God willing, would alter that.

Last night he had been reading in Mervyn Knight's recent publication from Longmans of London entitled: *Farms, Families and Dwelling Houses of Fermanagh*. He had read very closely about the dwelling and family he now approached.

CLONOULA	Meadow of apples or apple meadow
ASSOCIATED FAMILIES	One: WINTERS
LOCATION	Barony of Clanawley; Enniskillen, six miles, Tully Castle three miles, Dublin eighty miles.
SITUATION	Mountainside seven hundred and forty feet above sea level. Long view of Upper Lough Erne from eastside RV. £487.00
HISTORY	Held under chieftancy of Brian Maguire (disaffected) crown escheated 1610. Original house built by Thomas Winters under tenant of Sir John Hume of Tully Castle. Burned in 1641 rebellion. Rebuilt by Clement Winters 1660. Extended by Captain William Hudson Winters (sea) 1793. Gates, yard, gatelodge and the hamlet at Clonoula, etc.
PRESENT CONDITION	Good. Inhabited. Occupier: William Winters Esq.
SPECIAL FEATURES	Large cottage-type house, central chimneys, gabled bays. All windows have cutstone 'eyebrows'. Central doorway, pedimented with fanlight, spoiled by glass porch.
INTERIOR	One Adams-type fireplace, ceilings plain and low, pitchpine timber throughout. Otherwise unremarkable.
EXTERIOR	A sunken cobbled yard, walled garden and apple store (thatched) all built with random rubble. There is a lime kiln, scutch mill (in use), cornmill roofless. Original globe-topped piers

	in good order. Gatelodge occupied in good repair. Clonoula hamlet has four thatched cottages, one serving as a post office-cum-public house. There are two other cottages on the holding.
ASSOCIATED TENANT FAMILIES	Ruttledge, Ward, Blessing, McManus, Boyle, McCafferty.
ASSOCIATED TOWNLANDS	Ardnagashel . . . Height of forts Brackagh . . . A spreckled place Garvarry . . . Rough land Dacklin . . . A black meadow
GROUNDS	Well furnished with long-standing beech and oak. Orchard of twenty acres reputedly the oldest in Ulster. Avenue one thousand yards long steeply inclined towards the county road. This steep area a maze of thirty acres or more consists of hard woods, conifers and rhododendrons.

The Canon now paused on the avenue at an opening in this wooded area. He could see over and through a glory of rhododendrons the glittering map of Lower Lough Erne and its islands and, immediately below, the townlands of Brackagh, Garvarry and Dacklin, the black awkward landscape of the dispossessed. Hungry views and sour land can make the best people in the world sullen and dangerous. My people. Mister Knight's book could not say that Clonoula was an oddity amongst Fermanagh dwellings. Clearly its category was Protestant squireen, mock or low gentry. What it could not say was that Billy Winters had been married by Jimmy Donnelly, the present Catholic Bishop of Clogher who was at that time a boy curate in a country parish near Enniskillen, and he knew, like most others, that twenty-five years earlier, Billy Winters had gone drinking night and day for an extended period. Somewhere in the misery of his cups he had confided to a drunken comrade, or aloud to himself, 'Never cross the lough for a woman. Mine was served when I got her, three months gone.' And so the rumour spread about Fermanagh and neighbouring counties that one of the shrewdest young men in Ulster, the first man to build a macadamised road from his limestone quarries, a man who could hold his own with bishops and horse-dealers, who could teach tricks to tricksters, had himself been gulled and shamed by a woman, and worse again a Papist woman.

Thereafter Cathy Winters had lived on with him in the long farmhouse at Clonoula. During the twelve years that followed, it was said on and off: 'I see Billy's woman has a black eye' or 'that woman's aged a lot' and some said 'could you blame the man?' Others remarked 'He's a brute, the same Billy, a bad article, kicks and fists her about the house; it's thon Beth child I'd be sorry for, poor wee morsel.' And when Cathy Winters met with a sudden and terrible end in the yard at Clonoula, Billy stood over her grave with his arm around Beth sobbing in a way that was uncommon enough for those who witnessed it to say 'he must have loved her.' His own tribe were more suspicious: 'Thon wasn't for her, it was for Papist contracts. The man has no shame.' How much of this was true, false or malicious nonsense, he had no way of knowing. True or false, it was general knowledge.

Oddly, over the years when he called, it was Beth the solemn staring girl, now woman, who seemed watchful, distant in the presence of a priest, while Billy's manner was affable, open, avuncular, hospitable and on the surface civilised, and yes, there he was again, standing at the porch smiling, both arms extended momentarily in welcome. Referring to him last night the Bishop had said, 'I don't think Billy Winters believes in anything much apart from money and malt whiskey but he's straight, which is more than can be said for a lot of our crowd.'

Billy led the Canon's mottled grey mare and tied her alongside the porch to a limb of wistaria as the Canon dismounted saying:

'I have a letter for you here from James of Clogher.'

'Is it good or bad, Leo?'

'Haven't a notion but it must be urgent.'

They shook hands.

'You'll stay for a bite of breakfast?'

'I'll not, thank you, but I'll sit a minute. What a morning . . . thanks be to God.'

'It's the magic month,' Billy said.

'It's more to do with where you are,' the Canon said, 'up here, this place is half-way to heaven!'

A red setter came out of the rhododendrons and sat on the rectangle of gravel before the house, her tongue out panting, her copper coat shining in the sun:

'Is she new, Leo?'

'She is.'

'Any good?'

'It's too early to tell but she has a good nose and she's biddable.'

'It's the only way to have them.'

The Canon sat down on a bench in the porch placing his riding-crop on his knees. He then took out an envelope from the inner pocket of his frock-coat, handed it to Billy who sat facing him. Billy placed the letter on the windowsill behind.

It would have been, the Canon felt, more amicable if Billy Winters had opened the note, glanced at it and shrugged it off with a comment. On the other hand why should he? Opening it might have proved awkward. Could have been about me or God knows what. Bishops associate with very strange informants.

It seemed to Billy Winters that the parish priest was frowning at the tiled floor as though thinking of something unpleasant. The glazed tilework showed a beaver sitting on a log mid-river and underneath in Roman lettering three words in a semi-circle: Ī SEQUERE FLUMEN – follow the river. Billy waited for him to speak. When the silence continued he said:

'Nothing remarkable, Leo.'

'Yes and no . . . The Dummy McGonnell is back on his travels, we had him yesterday.'

'He's a harmless cratur,' Billy said.

'They should have kept him in Monaghan asylum.' He paused and then said with emphasis: 'One thing's certain, he didn't smash my new glasshouse.'

'By God! . . . when was this?'

'About midnight, Tuesday back.'

'And where where you?'

'Out in the jungle over by Brackagh Cross and Dacklin tryin' to put manners on the mad drinkers and devil-dancers.'

'Did you manage?'

'Oh I put them from it.' He raised his hunting-crop. 'With this.'

The lion of Dacklin. Well done Leo. The riding-crop for croppies. Small wonder they leave in droves for America, Australia, anywhere . . . lashing hell out of

24

what they can't have themselves ... or shouldn't ... better say something.

'The dancing's American,' Billy said.

'The liquor's local,' the Canon said, 'and puts them astray in the head.'

Startling images from three nights back reappeared in the Canon's mind. He had dismounted and crossed a braird of oats, green and thick as spring grass, then walked down a farm-pass through Dacklin towards Brackagh Cross. He could hear hand-clapping, a melodeon, the sound of laughter. There was a bright moon and he surprised a pair coupling in a dry sheugh, bare legs entwined cross-ankled round a man's thrusting body; blind moaning, both. He had lunged toward them, stumbling, roaring: 'beasts, brutes, devils', his bone-headed hunting-crop lashing the man's buttocks then flailing about his head and body as he backed away defending himself with one hand concealing his member with the other. He had turned then to punish the she-devil, but she had crept through the ditch and run across a field towards Brackagh Cross to warn the others. The melodeon, hand-clapping and laughter faded to a sudden silence under a full, chastened moon.

Billy Winters stared at the mild grey eyes, the saintly hair and the kind-seeming mouth. No hint of the brutal anywhere:

'Someone at the crossroads dance?'

'It was smashed when I got home ... It's Ward or Blessing, both your tenants.'

'You think?'

'I'm certain: it was one of the two, or both.'

The Canon tapped his riding-crop on his knee, began to say something, stopped and then said:

'You employ them, Billy.'

'No, no, they buy filler and stones at the quarry . . . it's the council pays them. Then of course *they* pay me.'

'It's your quarry.'

'True.'

'You could refuse them.'

Billy Winters was too startled to answer at once:

'I could . . . yes.'

'You should. Blessing is a wretched creature. Ward is worse; he's evil or near it.'

'He's full of himself to be sure . . . but evil, that's a big word, Leo.'

'Certainly he's a bad egg.'

During a pause the Reverend Leo McManus stared through the open porch door as a flurry of pigeons winged high from the beech trees. He followed their flight till they went out of vision.

'You'll have to explain to me why,' Billy said. The Canon hesitated and then said:

'I'm not at liberty to disclose.'

Moral Constabulary? Confessional secrets? Something more sinister?

'You do a lot of work for us here in Fermanagh, Billy . . . and all that marble-work in Monaghan Cathedral.'

'Is this a class of blackmail, Leo?'

'It's a request.'

Billy jerked his elbow in the direction of the Bishop's letter lying on the window-ledge behind him.

'Has this anything to do with it?'

'No, I'm very certain not.' After another brief pause the Canon said:

'You don't have to take my word.'

'I have no reason to doubt it,' Billy said, 'but I'll have to say why . . . to Ward.'

'At my *request* . . . he'll understand.'

Why Ward, Billy wondered? Son of a canal lock-keeper near Cootehill, orphaned early, more dragged up than reared by Old Tom Ward his poacher, poteen-making uncle at Brackagh; a spell at Florencecourt as an upgraded stable boy where there was talk of the big-house girls being too fond of the stable, and a question of theft; a while in the west with Boycott; then away to America for years and back now with this drawling talk; haulier, quack-doctor, notions of himself, hard to see why this priest was so extreme against him.

The brass tongue of the main door clicked and moved inwards and Mercy Boyle came into the porch carrying a tray covered with a lace cloth, three cups and a pot of coffee, a sugar bowl and a jug of cream. Mercy placed the tray on the bench alongside the Canon as he stood, muttering, 'Too much, too much, my own breakfast waiting, no call for all this bother,' mixed in with a greeting to Mercy, 'It is Mercy Boyle, isn't it . . . how are you Mercy?'

'I'm well, your reverence.' Beth held the door for Mercy to leave, closed it and moved to take the Canon's proffered hand.

'You can give her a double shake there,' Billy said, 'it's her birthday, and she saved a cow from bloat in the black dawn.'

Beth smiled back at the smiling men . . . two fathers . . . neither mine, she thought, as Billy rambled on, mock-ordinary with an avuncular Irishness, a manner he used with country priests, farm-hands and quarry workers, never with horse-Protestants or at the R.D.S.

She was pouring the coffee, aware from the nature of the silence that she had intruded on some private manner. She could see the letter addressed to

Billy, unopened, with the waxed, Episcopal seal of Clogher.

'And how,' asked her parish priest, 'do you propose to celebrate the day?'

Supposing they could mind-read . . . The thought was so bizarre it brought a faint flush to her cheeks as she said quickly:

'Making butter, bringing tea to the bog and there is a pig to be killed.'

'Who does that for you?' the Canon asked.

'Blinky Blessing,' Billy said.

'Ah.'

From the corner of her eye she could see Billy wink across at the parish priest.

'It'll not be all workaday, I have a surprise or two up my sleeve.'

And so have I, she thought, sitting with her cup alongside Billy. And I hope to God this man opposite doesn't start on now about family resemblances the way Old Lily Cole did once: mouth, nose, hands, eyes, voice, on and on, more painful for Billy than for me. From tomorrow on all that awkwardness would end forever.

Billy suddenly pointed a stubby forefinger at the Canon and said:

'You'll be at the Town Hall tonight, Leo?'

'That requires a dispensation and an early booking . . . I have neither.'

'Pity; I was at Trinity with him.'

'I didn't know you were a college man.'

'I am and I'm not . . . One year engineering, and then my father became sick . . .'

'So you know him?'

'*Knew* . . . Twenty-eight years ago . . . He was plain

Willy French then before he became the world-famous Percy French.'

There was a silence and Billy filled it by saying:

'I'm told he's a gifted painter.'

'A dead area for me . . . I'm colour-blind.'

'You can knock a snipe left and right, I've seen you; and drop a trout-fly on a saucer from twenty yards.'

The Canon smiled; pleased. Billy turned and said to Beth:

'It's a man like Leo you want, Beth, a keen sportsman, a good gardener, farmer and a sound Christian gentleman to boot, also he keeps bees . . . She's very choosy this one, I've brought them out here by the cartload; all sorts, overbred and underbred, young bucks and not so young, fellas in the bank, strong farmers, millers, merchants, apprentices to law, accountancy and architecture. She'll have nothing to do with any of them.'

'Nor they with me, Sir,' Beth said quietly.

'You give them no chance, girl.'

'You'll find the right man in your own good time,' the Canon said.

'I'm not looking,' Beth said, got up and walked with her cup of coffee from the porch to where the red setter was lying on the gravel. It stretched out its neck in shy greeting as she hunkered, stroking its head. Both men watched.

'You embarrassed her there, Billy.'

Billy Winters shook his head.

'She goes her own pad, you wouldn't have a notion what's in her head; her mother the same, you wouldn't know what's in any woman's head,' and then added, almost sourly, 'bar the obvious!'

The coupling image thrust itself into the priest's mind

and he wrenched away from it, frowning. Quaffing the rest of his coffee he stood up and said:

'I'll go, Billy.'

The red setter suddenly jerked up its head, ears cocked, head alert and staring over at the porchway. Without looking around Beth knew the priest must now be preparing to leave. She half-heard the exchange of banalities and the mock camaraderie camouflaging what she knew both felt about each other. Long ago, the bitter arguments with poor Mama. Why did he still pretend?

She waved to the departing priest who imparted his benediction, watched him for a moment leaving, the dog running in circles around the grey horse, and then went over to the porch where Billy was reading the Bishop's letter. He handed it to her without comment and she saw the Episcopal crest and the address.

> *Latlurcan House,*
> *Bishop's Residence,*
> *Dublin Road,*
> *Monaghan,*
> *Thursday, May 3rd, 1883*

Dear Billy,

A not so young man called Maurice Fairbrother called with us today. He had authority from Dublin Castle (Revenue Department) to look into our accounts. We obliged. He had a particular interest in all marble, masonry and stone-work supplied by you, and all monies, transactions exchanged. Father Benny Cassidy gave him a trunk full of papers all to do with the Cathedral and the cost of completion. He scarcely looked at them. We both thought he asked very few questions about what was supposed to be his interest.

Later I talked with him. His father is a steward at Chatsworth (Duke of Devonshire's seat) and so naturally we talked about the late Lord Frederick Cavendish and he became very affected when I expressed my very real horror at the manner of his brutal death in the Phoenix Park. Thereafter, he talked to me about matters privy (not secret) to the Crown and I of matters privy (not secret) to the Church. He has a good grasp of both. I can tell you he is no Revenue Commissioner but what he is, I know not. He asked about you in a way that I thought curious. He intends calling on you tomorrow. Like me I suppose you have learned long ago to expect the unexpected, to believe the incredible, to be wary of all men at all times.

I married you, I christened Elizabeth and we have been friends and you have dealt honestly with me down the years and I feel my impression of this man Fairbrother might prove helpful. By the way, how is Elizabeth? I hear she grows more and more like your poor Catherine. Tomorrow I go to Enniskillen to marry a niece and hope to enjoy an evening with Percy French. Will you be there? And Elizabeth? If not, my best regards, and if either of you are travelling this way be sure to call.

Yours sincerely in Christ,
James of Clogher +

P.S. Father Benny tells me there are some monies

outstanding. They will, Deo volente, be paid
before November ends. Jimmy.

As Beth handed the letter back to Billy she said:

'He's a Castle agent, Sir.'

'A spy?'

'Something like that.'

'What could he want with me; with us?'

'Information, that's their job.'

'He'll be in the wrong shop so.'

Billy stood looking at the letter, re-reading bits of it, and Beth ventured:

'Unless it could be to do with Mr Parnell staying here.'

'What bearing could that have?'

'Enough for the Castle to be curious.'

'To hell with it all; it's your birthday . . . let's go in and have breakfast, you've been up since black-dark.'

Billy folded the letter and put it in his waistcoat pocket, took Beth by the elbow and guided her down the hall toward the dining-room.

'Why didn't you wake me?'

'You were deep asleep, Sir.'

'Nonetheless.'

'Next time I will.'

'You're worth your weight in gold, girl.'

'Am I, Sir?' she asked.

May sunlight poured into the dining-room through the high windows, shining on the lead polish of the slate hearth and lighting the metal and glass on the rosewood dining-room table. Mercy had filled a large glass vase with rhododendrons, clematis and green fronds. She had set the table especially with white and blue ware and a good silver cutlery, and as they sat she placed before each a pan-fried breakfast and left a bowl of scones between them. Both thanked her and for a few minutes Billy questioned Beth for more details about the cow and the bloat, making her re-tell every detail step by step. As she answered, part of her mind became aware of another recent dawn and very different circumstances.

She had come down just before light, alerted by noise and clatter in the kitchen. Yes she could cut meat, yes she could butter bread, and while she did this, Billy had sat at the dining-room table splashing more whiskey onto the table than into his glass as he talked about travel and quarries and business and contracts all mixed with maudlin references to her mother. When it became tedious and incomprehensible, she moved to leave. He had gripped her thigh, his mouth opened foolishly and she remembered thinking 'If I had a gun now in the other hand, I could put it in his mouth and pull the trigger.' She kept looking steadily into his bloodshot eyes. He loosened his grip, swayed to his feet, 'Your legacy girl, your inheritance, all in that safe, waiting for you.' For a moment he stood as if undecided, looking from her face to the corner of the room. Then he was kneeling selecting the keys he kept clipped to his body night and day.

'Bring over that lamp.'

She carried over the oil lamp and held it up as he picked three keys. The first, a long iron key, opened the panelled door in the wainscoting; the second, a plug key, allowed a cast-iron door to slide sideways; then the one of the safe proper, an elegant two-sided brass key. The oiled tongue clicked within and there was a sense of weight as he turned the handle and the door swung open. The first thing she saw was the three-cornered beaver hat, like the one in the portrait of his grandfather, a swart-looking man holding a parchment in one hand, the beaver hat in the other. There was a scar running from the wintry left eye to the straight line of his upper lip; an Indian hatchet, Billy maintained. With a wheezy cackle he put the hat on his head and stared up at her: a latter-day likeness of the portrait merged with the knowing, grinning face of a drunkard.

There were rolled parchments, bundles of faded envelopes on open shelves, sandalwood caskets and mother-of-pearl boxes, a black log-book and a large bottom drawer the width of the safe. This he opened with a separate key which he took from within the safe. As he opened it with his left hand his right plunged into a glitter of gold coins. He took out a fistful, pulling off the beaver hat, and thrust them both up towards her and the light of the lamp.

'That's what helped put the shine on this place a hundred years ago ... French gold, the beaver loot of three million square miles.'

He nodded up towards the portrait, 'His motto, "Watch and seize."'

He wheezed out another coughing laugh and repeated, 'Watch and seize,' then, dropping his voice to a loud whisper, he said, 'And he did ... Look!'

Again he thrust the coins up into her face. She had stepped back startled, although long familiar with the mythology of the founding grandfather, and how he had signed up with the 'Company of Adventurers' in London in 1770, and sailed for Canada and Hudson Bay. She had heard tell of the white limbo of three million square miles where fur-traders made and lost fortunes, and took to whiskey and squaws. She knew of the brutishness of life and death out there, and how, that first winter, trekking up-river, their canoe had smashed on rocks, tumbling eight of them into the icy water. With all provisions lost, they had dug themselves in to await the return of the Cree Indian guide with food, clothing and help. One by one, over the next two days, his companions had died, in a cold so pitiless it could freeze quicksilver. Finally alone, after fighting off wolves and Arctic foxes attacking both the dead and the dying, he had shed bitter tears and closed his eyes – as he thought for ever – to open them in a smoky tepee under the warmth of a beaver blanket.

And how, in the years that followed, when war between England and France was almost continuous, an opportunity had presented itself. A French frigate and an English warship had been pounding each other with cannon fire round and round Hudson Bay since dawn. By noon the sides of both ships were so shattered the crews could see each other in the lower decks, as in an open-fronted dolls' house: priests and surgeons on both going about their duties in blood-stained aprons and surplices. Late that evening, tacking with guns faced away, the French captain called on the English captain to surrender. He refused, calling on the Frenchman to surrender. The Frenchman then sent for brandy to toast the courage of the Englishman, who sent for whisky to toast the courage of the Frenchman, and the battle continued. Watching this from the steps of a trading post with three comrades, Billy's grandfather said, 'We've watched enough: time to seize.' That night they loaded fifteen thousand beaver pelts into a sloop and sailed away to the north of France where they sold them for five boxes of gold; one for each of the crew, two for Captain Winters.

Suddenly, then, as though aware of what he was doing and saying, Billy replaced the gold and the beaver hat, locked the safe and, moving away from the corner, said almost matter-of-factly, 'If you mind your step, girl, bide your time, play your part,' he thumbed back in the direction of the corner, 'this could all be yours . . . this, and what I've added.'

The next morning he pretended to have forgotten everything. Was she to inherit? . . . and *how* mind her step? . . . submit while he over-stepped! And what part would she play? Bedmaker, shirt-washer, egg-boiler, stablegirl and dairymaid with Mercy Boyle to help? . . . probably live till he was ninety, might even marry again when she was long past childbearing.

She was re-filling the teacups when she heard Billy say now:

'Your parish priest had his new glasshouse smashed.'

'Mercy was telling me.'

'Was she there? At the crossroads? Drinking and devil-dancing?'

Beth heard her own laugh mixed in with Billy's chuckle as she said:

'Such a shame, where else can they meet . . . ?'

'He hunted them with his riding-crop; did Mercy mention that?'

He watched her face for reaction; none. The haunted face of an insomniac, darkish rings under her eyes, red-brown hair Gretel-plaited, and a full mouth so like Cathy's, it was heart-wrenching. All through breakfast she gave the impression of being remote, almost unlistening, yet she had been out across fields and down the yard, and helping to prepare breakfast:

'You're tired Beth . . . you must be.'

36

'Not very, Sir.'

'You slept well.'

'Until the beast woke me.'

'You should have woken me.' Her mouth shaping words, her mind elsewhere, Billy noticed; thinking what?

'Leo say's he knows the blackguard.'

'Yes?'

'Our near-neighbour and tenant ... Liam Ward. Thinks he's evil.'

'Evil, Sir?'

'That's the word he used.'

'In what way?'

'He refused to say ... confessional stuff.'

'I doubt if Ward confesses, I've never seen him in Church.'

'Maybe his ladies confess; if you could call his consorts "ladies".'

'Would that make him evil, Sir?'

'His exact words were, "he's a bad egg ... near evil".'

Beth thought about this, then said:

'I suppose most humans are, more or less ... this way or that.'

What was she implying? Sensing accusation, his mind sought and found an answer.

'There's foolishness,' Billy said, 'and there's evil.'

After the drunken night and the beaver gold, he had talked the following morning at breakfast about malt whiskey being 'an awful man', about 'falling into bad company' in Enniskillen and that he 'couldn't remember a damnation thing; nothing; lucky to have a big pony like Punch who could find his way home in the dark.'

She knew then and he half or wholly knew what had happened. Often growing up she would say aloud 'I wish he was dead.' Sometimes, half-awake, half-asleep, it calmed her to plan his death, push him from the quarry edge, spike his whiskey with poison or – the terrible answer she had read in Carleton – set the house on fire when he was in a deep drunken stupor and watch from the ring-fort, the kyle or the fountain hill . . . burning, burning, burning away the wrongdoing of the past; retribution, not vengeance. The impossibility, the awfulness of such actions made dreaming of them a kind of exhilarating solace.

As they ate scones with butter and marmalade, Billy got up during a silence, went over to the sideboard and took an envelope out of the drawer. Out of it he then slipped what looked like a ticket, and placed it before her. She read:

MR PERCY FRENCH
OF WORLD RENOWN
WILL SING HIS INIMITABLE SONGS
AND RECITE HIS FAMOUS RECITATIONS
AT THE TOWN HALL
ENNISKILLEN
ON THURSDAY 3RD OF MAY 1883
TIME: 7 P.M.

Silly ballads, banjos, idiot recitations of wretched doggerel which she found unfunny and all of it spiced with a painful sentimentality. Every other public house in the country and many private ones reverberated with drunken renderings. To have to listen to the creator of such stuff singing them in public would be a kind of torture. In any case she couldn't go. For weeks the imagining of this coming night had filled her mind night and day. She heard herself say:

'I don't much care for Percy French, Sir.'

'You don't like Percy French?'

'No, Sir.'

'What don't you like about him?'

'The silliness I think . . .'

Billy's hand came out and retrieved the ticket slowly as he repeated, 'Silliness?'

'Yes, Sir.'

'All the world is singing his songs . . . is the whole world silly?'

Silly seemed to her now a kind word for what the world considered wonderful:

'I don't care about what he does.'

'What do you care about?'

'John Keats.'

'And what does he sing about?'

She paused, thinking, then said: 'Death and night-ingales.'

'Maybe he'll come and warble for us in the Town Hall sometime.'

'You *know* he's dead and gone, Sir.'

'Where no birds sing.'

'If you can quote him, why pretend?'

'Because I know and like Percy French; it's your birthday . . . it's an outing. But no matter, I can find someone for your ticket.'

Her mother all over again . . . punishing . . . not dislike of Percy French; dislike of anything I like.

Beth had known for years that Billy had known Percy French as a student. He would sit in the front row of the Town Hall, clap too loudly and afterwards very likely bring her backstage to meet Mr French. Then the probability of drunken groping on the way back in the gig, the stumbling and mumbling as he unharnessed the colt in the yard, the obligatory piano recital and singing. All this he would have to do on his own tonight while the heart-chilling plan with Ward would begin. Thereafter she would be gone from here forever, and ever and ever and ever . . . Amen.

'You're missing a rare chance.'

'I dislike concerts, Sir . . . I thought you knew that.'

'You seemed to go every other week in Italy.'

'That was opera.'

'You'll be alone here.'

'With fowl in the yard and the fields full of sheep and cattle and crows and pigeons, thousands of them, and all the swallows now and a corncrake who never stops and when he does a donkey starts. It's the least lonely place in the whole world.'

'It's good to see you smile, Beth, I thought maybe you were out of sorts about something.'

'I'm content enough, Sir.'

'Then we'll mark your birthday some other way, some other day.'

'That would be nice, Sir.'

'You won't change your mind?'

'I'd rather not go.'

He had been moving towards the door and then opened it slightly, hesitating, listening as voices came through from the kitchen. Beth could half-hear and rec-ognise Jim Ruttledge's slow guttural voice, all laughing when Mercy's brother Gerry rhymed something. Then Mickey Dolphin giving a detailed account of how he had once trekked up to the lough field, the canula going in 'lek a whiplash', the hiss of trapped gas, and laughter as

Gerry stammered out an inanity. Then Mickey talking through him, saying 'I wouldn't tangle with Miss Beth if she'd that yoke in her pocket; she could do harm, she could puncture a body badly.' Then Jim Ruttledge's deep voice: 'What about Mercy here, could you be punctured Mercy?'

In an eruption of good-natured laughter and banter, Mercy could be heard saying, 'Lek a pack of silly wee boys, the whole lot of ye!'

Billy half-smiled, blinking over at Beth, cleared his throat and went through to the kitchen. A sudden silence, then a gradual pick-up in talk. She could hear Billy saying:

'The Canon tells me the Dummy McGonnell is prowling the country again. Do you know him, Gerry?'

'I do, Sorr.'

Gerry Boyle, Mercy's brother, had the same large, dark, staring eyes as his sister. He listened to everything with his mouth open, showing gapped teeth, and when he did speak it was to stammer out a rhyme or folk maxim he had memorised. 'A wee want, poor fella,' kindly people said. He was mostly described, though, as 'an eejit'.

'Deed and I do, Sorr; he, he, he scars weemen, and he's fierce strong, he, he, he, hisses at them like a goose, and that frights them tarror to give him all about the place ... he's a class of harmless rogue, Sorr.'

'I'm sure,' Billy said, 'and smokes that pipe of his in every barn he's let into ... trail of barn-fires after him. I don't want him next or near the place and if he gets contrary send for me, I'll deal with him.'

As Beth put the breakfast dishes on the dining-table she could hear them talking about the bog, turf-cutting and the weather, heard Billy tap the barometer and talk about change and Mickey Dolphin saying, 'The paper give it good all this week,' and Jim Ruttledge saying, 'How would you know that Mickey, you can't read.' Then the men all leaving the kitchen.

She went through to the kitchen with the breakfast dishes, then out to the scullery where Mercy was placing his lunch in a black leather bag as she did every weekday morning: rasher sandwiches wrapped in damp butter muslin, a slice of caraway-seed cake and a sauce bottle of cold tea. Billy Winters looked out the scullery window at the three men crossing the yard as though trying to remember something. Twenty-five years ago on this day and about this time, he had heard an infant's cry coming down the well of the staircase, mixed with old Doctor McAllister's voice talking to the midwife. Overwhelmed he had left uncertain of where he was going or how long he would stay away. Here, now, the same green eyes looking from the same face, a living portrait of treachery? Beth was replacing the canula that she had washed and scalded in the drawer of the veterinary press. What to say? how to say it? He moved towards her, took her elbow and steered her toward the back door. He opened it, stepping out onto dry cobbles under cloudy sunlight and the sudden high skreek of early swallows:

'Seems poor enough some way . . . your birthday.'

'I'm content, Sir, truly.'

'With this house, these fields . . . not me.'

'Sometimes.'

'Say what it is that has you moody?'

'Now?'

'Yes, let's hear and be done with it. You bear me some resentment.'

Beth felt suddenly tired of pretending and said:

'I think you know, Sir, and I know you know.'

'I've never harmed you, Beth.'

In the silence that followed, the corncrake on the fort hill began a far-away coda.

'Have I?'

'I don't know, Sir.'

'I'd rather die than harm you, girl ... you know that.'

'Do you really want to hear.'

'Yes.'

'The last time you came in and sat in my bed, kissed me, not fatherly, said then something I'd rather not repeat. That's when I got angry, Sir, and went to sleep in Mercy's bed.'

'Oh God,' Billy groaned, 'what stuff to launch a sunny day in May?'

'You wanted to hear, Sir.'

He moved across the yard, turned and said:

'The day did start well though, you did well and I'll be mindful of that.'

Beth shook her head and shrugged trying to find words to conclude the encounter:

'It's what anyone would have done, Sir.'

'We'll talk again,' Billy said, 'I'll make amends.'

Too late, Beth thought, watching him walk after Mickey Dolphin with his two white enamel buckets which he used to fetch spring water for the house every morning from a surface spring-well half-way to the quarry. The water flowing through the yard from the fountain hill had an amber tinge and a boggy taste.

In dry weather, summer or winter, Billy Winters preferred to walk to the quarry. There was a great deal more to see: cattle, sheep and, at the moment, the orchard in blossom – and always the view of the Lower Lough as he approached the quarry. It was also a mile shorter on foot than going down the avenue in the gig to the county road and then round to the quarry. Billy now walked on under the arched entry and down the back lane picking his steps carefully to avoid cow-dung on his fine leather boots. Mickey Dolphin, hearing him, turned and stopped, waiting. As Billy Winters approached he kept looking at the sky and it seemed to Mickey Dolphin that his master's face was fixed in anger:

'What can you read up there, Mr Billysorr?'

'It tells me you were drunk last night and very likely still are . . . You'll be got dead some morning, and no one to bury you.'

Billy Winters did not hesitate and walked on past Mickey who picked up his buckets and went half-running after him:

'You'd bury me, Billysorr.'

'Why should I?'

'You're fond of me, a track.'

'Why should I be . . . what have you ever done this thirty years but take wages for doing sweet bugger-all.'

'Wages, Billysorr . . . ten shillings a month?'

'Aye, and the run of your teeth, a roof over your head and my old shirts and boots and woollens.'

'You're horrid cross this morning, Billysorr.'

Billy suddenly shouted:

'Four men: you, me, Gerry Boyle and Jim Ruttledge and a cow blaring out her trouble and who saves her from the bone-yard? Not me, not you, not Gerry, not Jim Ruttledge but a slip of a girl, Elizabeth Rosaleen.'

'Aye, Miss Beth, she's a wonder, that girl. And sure the cow's alive and well, Sorr.'

'Will you tell me,' Billy said in a measured voice, 'what's wrong with Mr Percy French? You're a balladeer, you play the mouth organ, you're a ceilidh and crossroads man, a foot-tapping jigger, a poteen guzzler; you tell me, Mickey Dolphin, what is wrong with Mr Percy French?'

'Not a hate wrong with him, Sorr ... by all accounts.'

'Then you leave the bog at five, shave and put on your best wearables and have Punch harnessed and ready to leave at six. You'll hear Mr French in the Town Hall tonight.'

Billy suddenly stopped and put his left hand out to stop Mickey, his right finger going up to his lips to enjoin silence. They stood listening at a point where the farm-pass to the quarry fell away two graves deep to an acre of cut-over bog, a wilderness of birch, alder and sycamore where the refuse from Clonoula had been tipped and buried, topped up and overgrown, time out of mind, pram-wheels and cart-wheels, hoops, rotten barrels and bins, shards of vessels and crockery, rusting storm-lamps all mixed up with builders' debris, lath and plaster, discarded invoices and ledgers and, grotesquely, a blind doll grinning sideways from a recent heap.

In the silence they could hear what seemed like a steady snoring. Billy pushed his way down through dead bracken and briar till they got to the bog floor. Freckled light, dim as a cathedral and away in the middle of this they saw the Dummy McGonnell asleep, his head pillowed on bracken fronds in the fork of a birch tree on what looked like an island surrounded by the blackness of gleaming bog-holes. 'The Dummy,'

Billy whispered to Mickey, who said, 'He'll hardly start a fire in here, Sorr.'

After a minute their eyes became adjusted to the dim light and Mickey asked:

'Would a body be better blind or deaf in this world?'

'Deaf,' Billy said. 'What you hear is worse than what you see.'

'I'd liefer be blind a hundred times; blind.'

It was then that Billy Winters became aware that Mickey Dolphin had begun to tremble, his narrow head jerking his fringe like a mop on a mechanical toy. He did not see that Mickey's gaze had shifted from the blind doll on the refuse heap to the white face of a drowned child staring up through the brown water of the bog-pool. Billy looked down into the water. He could see nothing and whispered urgently:

'What's wrong with you man?'

The crying, when it came, was from within; a nasal whine so painful that Billy moved away a few yards, embarrassed and muttering, 'You'll have to quit the "singlings", Mickey, no man's a match for raw poteen.'

He then saw Mickey Dolphin kneeling, staring into a bog-pool, tears plashing down through his fingers:

'Jesus Christ,' Billy muttered, 'what *is* all this?' He went over and hunkered beside Mickey putting an arm around his shoulder:

'It's all right Mickey. I was joking; we'll bury you proper.'

'No odds how I'm buried.'

The sobbing then changed to something between giggling and laughing. It stopped as suddenly as it had begun with Mickey sitting back on his heels, wiping his face.

The Dummy suddenly sat up, looking across at the two men, one kneeling, one hunkered. He half-growled, bent over the water in front of him, covered his face with his hands and began whining in what seemed like an imitation of Mickey's grief. Billy said:

'Leave him be, don't look at him.' Taking Mickey by the arm, he steered him up out of the bog onto the farm-pass.

'What were you looking at down there?'

Mickey Dolphin shook his head.

'You're going astray in the head, Mickey.'

'Aren't we all a track that way,' Mickey said, and when he began to tremble again Billy Winters took him by the shoulders, turned him and pointed him towards the well saying:

'Fetch your water; be ready at six.'

As he watched Mickey go down the path to the well under the mountain ash he heard the Dummy coming out of the bog, a rope closing his long button-less coat, a great bone-headed man with three large yellow teeth in his top gums, a scissored stubble and blood-veined eyes.

He came shambling down the farm-pass in two odd boots making sign language. Trying to avoid involvement, Billy Winters kept saying:

'All right, all right.'

The Dummy blocked his path shaking his head, forcing Billy to look at his mouth which was saying:

'I'm not all right . . . I'm hungry.'

'Go up to the house so,' Billy said; 'they'll give you breakfast . . . And no malingering in the yard after; and no sleeping in lofts or haysheds.'

The Dummy growled, twitching up his nose as though smelling something unpleasant:

47

'And who in hell are you, McGonnell,' Billy asked, 'to mock at Mickey Dolphin?'

The Dummy glared from angry eyes shaking his head and pursing his lips. Billy persisted:

'He was distressed and you mocked him.'

The Dummy shook his head in strong disagreement. By sign and gesture, his hand on his heart, he conveyed that Billy had mistaken mockery for sympathy.

'And what could you know about Mickey Dolphin? He's been with me twenty-five years.'

With a knowing grin the Dummy conveyed that he knew almost everything about everybody.

He then put his hand deep in his coat pocket and pulled out the stub of an indelible pencil. On the soft white palms of his work-shy hand, he drew a rough half-circle. Within this he pencilled the image of a child lying on its back at the bottom of the circle.

'A womb?' Billy asked, placing a hand on his own rib-cage. The Dummy shook his head. He pointed to the path where Mickey Dolphin had gone down with the buckets, went on his hunkers and described a circle on the ground with his forefinger.

'A well?'

The Dummy nodded. Using his thumb he then sketched a face with a fringe like Mickey's, daubing tears and bending his thumb to show a figure kneeling and weeping over a well.

'A drowned child?' The Dummy nodded.

'Mickey's?'

Again he nodded, and began to elaborate. Mickey had gone to a spring well one evening with his little girl. He was drunk, fell asleep, and woke up to find his child staring up at him from the bottom of the well. His wife went off her head and left him for a neighbour man. Mickey drank more, was evicted, and took to the roads and that's how the Dummy had met him long, long ago in the County Tyrone.

'Better blind than deaf,' Billy muttered as the Dummy now proffered a begging hand.

'Beggary, for what?' Billy asked.

The Dummy rubbed the thumb and forefinger of his right hand together. He then joined his hands and placed them against his right cheek and closed his eyes.

'Money for lodgings,' Billy muttered. 'Dumb you might be, McGonnell, but you're an artful class of a beggar.'

He placed a shilling in the Dummy's hand and set off along the farm-pass leading to the quarry and as he walked, Billy Winters was thinking of treacherous wombs and treacherous wells and how everyone, less or more, has some shameful and painful secret to conceal. On the path leading to the spring-well he could see Mickey Dolphin's slight figure stooping for water. What was his toddler called? A little girl; Christ in heaven, her name must be graven on his heart. Did God grin down on that, too? Suffer the little ones. Clobbers all of us this way or that. Crawling, running, shuffling till lights out and the Prince of Glory or the other fella; or nothing!

The land began to slope down toward the Lower Lough. He could now see the familiar square tower and the roof-shapes of the crushing mill and riddle house and heard the skreeking noise of a steel drill-bit going down into the limestone. Forty holes would have to be drilled deep for the dynamite arriving at midday from Enniskillen under heavy guard in a sealed carriage. He became aware of Donnelly's letter: 'Expect the unexpected . . . be wary of all men at all times.' Was there something unsaid? He could ask him tonight in the Town Hall.

Nearing the edge of the quarry he paused at the top of a stone staircase leading down to the office. On good days like this he could see back to the spires and tower of Enniskillen Town Hall, and make out the county roads and by-roads, the avenues and mansions, the cottages dug into the landscape. For almost a hundred years this lough-side quarry had helped supply the stones that built them, the filler and gravel that paved them.

There was a pyramid of fist-sized rubble beside the crusher. Beyond it were three acres of hacked grey-black limestone, the dried-up pools and paths rutted by slipes, carts and drays, which led to the far end of the quarry where, outside a large slated stone shed, there were tombstones, altars, a half-finished pulpit and marble fireplaces in various stages of completion. On the gable of the shed in bold capitals it said:

WINTERS' MONUMENTAL WORKS

Years ago one of the Adamsons murmured, 'Have we a Michelangelo here in West Fermanagh?' High gentry very grand about trade. A tombstone-maker one step above an undertaker. In less than fifteen years the same man had squandered his paintings, sculptures, and marble staircase, his lands now reverting to cattle jobbers, rushes and ragwort. Billy's father had once said, 'Unless they have old money or marry new money or learn to trade like us they'll disappear. Take care, son, and mind the old money, add to it and be kind to the land. That way you survive.'

He had followed this advice, though solvency seemed pointless when everything in time would pass to indifferent kin: two married female cousins and their families near Dungannon. Who would then control and direct the work of this quarry, the farm and all that entailed? Was the codicil unfair to Beth? Old Patterson, coldly legal and sharply personal: 'A will is about what you want, Sir, and of course the girl is deserving; but if you go first she could marry one of her own. And what then? Did we cross the sea and fight for that? Have we wrought here three hundred years to have it taken from us that way? No, Sir, you must be clear about what happens when you are gone. With respect, you made one blunder; do not compound it with another.'

Far below, beyond the dust and clamour of the quarry, the levelness of the lough seemed fixed in a strike of sunlight so blinding he could scarcely make out the shape of Corvey Island and Tirkennedy beyond it.

4

Beth had gone up to her bedroom with the brass bed, the woodwormed floor, the ewer and the basin with its painted daffodils. Outside the window under the overhang she had almost ceased to hear a family of starlings, there since childhood; noisy, garrulous, friendly.

One case was already packed. The second contained shoes, some books and a few toilet things. This case was half-empty. She opened it and picked up Jane Austen, Emily Brontë, Dickens and William Carleton. A card used as a marker fell to the ground, a photograph of archaeological excavation at Pompeii. Replacing it in a book she became aware of forgotten correspondence under newspaper lining in a chest of drawers. She removed a bundle of linen, lifted out the newspaper uncovering envelopes of different sizes. She then replaced the newspaper and linen and sat on the bed, glancing at sentences, half-reading notes, letters and cards. One bundle was marked 'Mam'. As she put it in the case an image came back of her mother saying:

'If I happen to go first . . . Don't lay me out in my wedding dress . . . use the one with the lace collar, the

53

green one . . . and make sure my own name is on the stone: Maguire.'

What an image to return now. She could feel her eyes swimming as she methodically tore up the rest of the correspondence. A note from Ward she put in the pocket of her dress. A letter she had received in Castel de Cortese near Naples she now found herself reading quickly and then re-reading. Written two years ago, it was from Billy Winters.

> *Clonoula,*
> *August 9th, 1881*

My Dear Elizabeth,

> *Now I begin to see the*
place you describe. Naples is a very long way
from home.

You ask me for news. It's quiet here mostly.
Yesterday I rowed out to Corvey, your island.
The business of punting cattle out and back to
thirty unmannered acres is a doubtful one. Today
I posted to Enniskillen for Matthew Gemmel's
funeral. He cut his throat poor fellow. Loneliness,
the minister said. Again there are rumours afloat
that I am to sell Clonoula, that the quarry is
bankrupt and that I have become an inveterate
night tippler. All wishful talk from my well-wishers
hereabouts!

Our meadows are all scythed, saved and stacked
in the barns, lofts and haggard; about three
hundred rucks in all. The yard smells sweet and
summery. Our cattle will be content this winter.

Soon I'll have hooks out to the barley and
pullers out to the flax. Did I tell you I tried out a

field of linseed? It flowers blue like the grotto at Capri you wrote me about. People stare at it. It's worth coming back to Fermanagh to view such a wonder: a blue field under a black sky.

Let me say now that I would love to see you home again. I can give you a few good reasons for returning. Firstly you belong here, you play the piano well and sing sweetly when persuaded! For the six months you were here, you managed the yard and dairy better than any working steward. Every room in the house is missing your presence! Will you think about this? I promise to conduct myself as honourably as any man in Ulster. Do you believe me? Do I believe myself? Absolutely.

The new dispensary doctor is a young man called Bell. I called on him after Gemmel's funeral. He tells me my chest pains are 'intercostal neuritis' and that I'm as healthy as a goat. I think you'd like him, a quirky sense of humour, a real Ulsterman.

I grow benign with the years believe me, and every day I miss you.

> You have at all times my deepest love,
> Papa

Could anything be more genial. 'You belong here'; 'Every day I miss you'; 'At all times my deepest love'.

She was uncertain what to do about the letter; she placed it in her pocket, took it out and replaced it in the case, took it out again and then slowly began to tear it in small pieces aware as she did so of Mercy's footsteps on the staircase, then her voice:

'Are you up there, Miss?'

'I am, Mercy, yes . . .'

'Would you like me to scrub out the kitchen or start straight in to churn?'

'The churning, Mercy, I'll be down in five minutes.'

Some time today she would have to tell Mercy she would be leaving here at dawn tomorrow; for good, most likely. That would be difficult. Meantime she would have to behave as naturally as possible.

She continued to destroy the correspondence, occasionally tearing out an address which she placed in the open case. She then closed the case, put it under the bed and went down with the paper debris and funnelled it into the kitchen stove. When it was burning well she left the kitchen, through the pantry to the back hall and out to the cobbled yard.

She could hear from the dairy opposite the back door the rhythmic splatter of Mercy churning.

In the cool, sour smell of the flagged dairy Mercy was plunging the churnshaft up and down to a rhyme she heard at home:

'Come butter, come butter, come butter, come;

Every lump as big as my bum.'

Beth moved now to relieve her:

'It's small lumps we'd have Mercy to match your bottom.'

'Oh God, thanks Miss, I'm wringin' wet, soaked through . . .'

Mercy went over and leaned against a wide slate shelf with its crocks full of buttermilk, skimmed milk, whey, and cheeses wrapped in muslin. She took a handful of ragged muslin from a box and began wiping her face, neck and arms as she watched Beth continue the churning. A kind mistress to work for, a bit stand-offish, or shy or something, but a picture to look at: her strong arms working the shaft, her blouse tightening and loosening to the movement, the Parnell locket swinging rhythmically. Spiteful catty ones said the Winters girl was platter-faced, and she was a bit maybe, but her skin was beautiful – and her eyes. And her voice was lovely – throaty, sort of – and when she laughed it was so merry she was like someone else. But it was hard to make her laugh. Why were there so few men callers? Did she frighten them off? Too educated? Polite and proper? The way just now she said 'bottom' instead of 'bum', 'arse', or even 'backside', and the way she was so nice about the locket. Mercy could tell she didn't really like it; which was hard to make out, because almost everyone in Ireland was ready to die for Mr Parnell. And the way she keeps on trying to get me to talk her way: to say 'did' instead of 'done'. There was a near fight about that one day; Mercy had cried and Beth hadn't corrected her since. Odd hours they did reading and writing together and Beth had shown her how to make Clones Lace. Mercy was grateful and counted herself one of the luckiest girls in Fermanagh.

In less than ten minutes the cream had turned to crumbly butter. In the silence of the work that followed – kneading, scalding, salting and shaping – they heard the stone-crusher grinding to a stop in the quarry below. Half an hour later the lumbering steel-shod wheels of Ward's draycart could be heard coming down the county road from the townland and tenancy of Brackagh.

'That's Liam Ward's dray,' Mercy said. Beth did not respond.

'The fellas goin' now is . . . a bad lot mostly.'

'In what sense, Mercy?'

'Well, the ones you'd meet at a dance or a cei-lidh . . . they've no notion how to talk to a girl, less manners nor a dog, they've no . . .' Mercy searched for the word, could not find it, and shrugged, 'They have . . .'

'No gentleness?' Beth suggested.

'It's up against a wall they want you or down in a ditch, and no talk.'

'All of them?'

'I've never met one of them not like that.'

'And your Mayo friend Constable Shanley?'

'Oh, he's afeared of his shada that fella, a gossipy auld woman, "information" is all he's after, and I told him things I shouldn't have.'

'You did?' Beth said. 'Like what?'

She could see the momentary embarrassment in Mercy's face.

Coming home late from a crossroads dance Mercy had been drawn to the dining-room by the lighted window and the sound of piano-playing. Looking in she had seen Beth playing, the boss standing behind her, his hands resting on her shoulders, the tips of his fingers close to her breasts. Mercy could tell from Beth that she was either afraid or in a temper, or both. She had crept in the back door and lay listening, and heard talking in the bedroom across the corridor. Then, after a while, Beth came in and got in beside her. Mercy pretended to be asleep and though she made no sound she could sense that Beth was crying.

'Like what?' Beth asked again.

'Like telling him about Biddy O'Gorman, the way she was big as a haystack one day and all of a shot she was thin as a rake and nothing to show for it. There was talk. Some said it was born dead and others that it was made to die; you know the blather and spite they go on with about here. Then the day after I told Seamus Shanley the Constabulary came and searched O'Gorman's. They found nothin'. He must've squealed.'

'God help her,' Beth said.

'The devil mend the men,' Mercy said. 'Tommy O'Hara, Willie Dawson, Liam Ward, and God knows who else. She was a giddy thing, Biddy, man-giddy.'

Alerted to hear Ward's name, Beth turned away from Mercy's eyes. Mercy was glad. She *had* told Shanley about the night scene and the piano, and sensed afterwards that *he* had probably told Sergeant Cassidy. And if Cassidy knew, Inspector Quinn knew, and Dublin Castle knew; that made her an informer by accident.

Albert, a sixteen-week-old pig, was fed skimmed milk by Mercy for the last time as Beth scalded the churn, dash and butter makers, then placed them to air in a flyproof cabinet.

Crossing the yard towards the kitchen, she said:

'I might go up and rest a while, Mercy.'

'And why not . . . you've been up half the night . . . better again you'll miss Blinky Blessing cuttin' poor Albert's throat!'

'Can you manage on your own?'

'I've seen it too often, Miss. When it's over I'll call you . . . we can take tea to the bog together.'

They crossed the yard, filled and carried a basket of logs from the corner of the turf shed. As Mercy loaded the fire-box of the stove Beth came in from the pantry with two glasses of lemonade. She placed one on the table then stood looking out of the window to the yard, as though alone. When she left without a word Mercy went out to the hall and called up the staircase:

'Take a good rest for yourself, Miss.'

Beth's voice came down remote from the upper hall:

'Yes, thank you, Mercy.'

Mercy stood listening till she heard the click of the bedroom door. Quare and moody today and it her birthday. Funny feeling in the dining-room at breakfast, both falling over each other to thank me for filling a teapot. Is the boss up to his old tricks or some new ones, and what did I blurt about Shanley? 'Told him things I shouldn't have' . . . and the steady way then she looked and looked till I blushed up. Janey Mack I wouldn't harm her for all the oats in Ulster! She knows that, fonder of her than any fella, and ten times more than Shanley, with his bare-faced lies. 'Twas a neighbour says he split on Biddy O'Gorman. Liar! The worst neighbour ever wouldn't tell on a girl in trouble that way, not hereabouts. Shanley it was, for certain sure. He'll rise high in the world that fella, crown-shawning round the clergy and the Crown. Bad cess to the day I met him, full of himself with the full of his drawers. At least I didn't let him that night, nor any other. Imagine having a baba like him, may God forgive me. I'd drown it before I'd rear it, the toady face and the moany noise of him, asking me was it real silver here in the house or the pretend stuff, and what was the maker's name on the good Delft? How in God's name would a girl like me know the like of that. And what sort of man would want to know the like! An auld woman and sneaky along with it. I'm well shot of him.

Mercy drank her lemonade and went out to the round steel tub in the yard to wash and prepare potatoes for the main meal of the day.

5

The look-out-cum-office was perched half-way up the quarry at the top of a limestone staircase. Its dusty gable window looked down on a view of the lower lake and islands and across to Tirkennedy. Directly below, Billy could see Ward's draycart with its two grey geldings clattering through the entrance. Blessing was sitting alongside him:

'That's Ward and Blessing,' Billy said.

R.I.C. Inspector Joseph Quinn came over, stood alongside Billy and looked down:

'An unholy brace of hoeboys,' he said.

He was a dark grey-faced Mayo man with a jutting mouth. Every Christmas, Billy gave him a box of apples and a bottle of whiskey. They understood each other very well. Tommy Martin, seated at a high clerk's desk in the corner, muttered:

'Steal the winkers from a nightmare ... if they were let.'

Far below, on the floor of the quarry, men signalled with their arms up to stop Ward's horses, some pointing to the quarry top where a steel rig was drilling the last of three dozen forty-foot holes ten feet back from the quarry face. Constable Seamus Shanley and two other policemen were supervising and checking the unloading of dynamite delivered two hours earlier by steel coach from the railway station at Enniskillen.

'How many men have you watching?' Billy asked.

'What you see . . . and three lads you can't see.'

'A waste of time,' Tommy Martin said.

'You think?' Quinn asked.

'The guts of four thousand sticks to pack into them holes . . . they'll be all day at it, up and down with boxes filling and tamping and firming every hole. I don't care how many men you have watching . . . they'll nick a few unbeknownst to anyone . . . Am I right, boss?'

Billy shrugged.

'How? We can count, and we're not blind.'

'You can watch and watch and still be codded,' Tommy said, and then nodded towards Ward and Blessing.

'That pair down there . . . who in hell could watch the like of them?'

Billy turned to Quinn:

'Do you want to talk to him now about the glass-house thing?'

The Inspector shook his head.

'We've nothing to go on . . . he gets up to all his capers in the dark, you'd have to be an owl to catch him'.

'A born trickster,' Tommy Martin agreed.

Billy Winters went out into the May sunlight, cupped his hands and shouted down:

'Ward!'

Ward looked up. Billy beckoned with a wave of his right arm and watched as Ward came up the stairway,

conscious that his movements were more cat- than carter-
like. Billy went through to his office, pulling at his nose
talking back over his shoulder:

'I have this small problem, Liam.'

'You'll solve it, Mr Winters.'

As Ward followed Billy into the office, he saw the
uniform, engaged Quinn's eyes for a second:

'The law's high up today!'

When Quinn did not respond, Ward said:

'And how is Inspector Quinn?'

'Biding my time, son.'

'Trouble growing in the fields?'

'A lot of noxious weeds about; we'll deal with them.'

Billy interposed.

'I had a visit this morning, Liam, from your parish
priest.'

'*Your* friend, Leo McManus.'

'Client, Liam, I have no friends, no enemies, just
clients . . . what did you do on him?'

The pause extended unnaturally until Ward asked:

'What's he saying?'

'He's saying he'll cancel all orders from this quarry
for the church avenue if I hire you to deliver . . . that's
what he's saying'.

'Jesus,' Ward muttered.

'Mind your language, Ward,' the Inspector said.

'Is it aginst the law now to say "Jesus"?'

'I'm cautioning you, boy.'

'You're a caution all right.'

'What did you do on him?' Billy asked again.

'You tell me . . . I haven't a pup's notion.'

'He broke up a crossroads dance and someone broke
up his new glasshouse before he got back . . . He thinks
it was you.'

'He could be right,' Tommy Martin muttered.

'Stick to you sums, Tommy,' Ward said.

'Was it?' Billy asked.

'If I wanted to harm the man, I could think of something better or worse.'

'I'd be certain of that,' Quinn said.

'Well that's it Liam,' Billy said, 'you can't supply for the avenue at Tully but the county roads go on forever . . . you'll not be stuck for work.'

Billy turned to Tommy Martin and said:

'Give him a chit for that new stretch out by Dernagola.'

Ward took the piece of paper, looked at it and began moving towards the door. With his back to the three men he said:

'He'll be sorry.'

Billy directed his voice to Ward's back:

'"The man Ward is bad", your priest said, "near evil".'

Ward turned at the door. The three men watched the effect on his face: none.

'That fellow would turn me into a rabbit,' Ward said, 'roast me for his dinner if he could . . . That's evil . . . tell him that from me.'

Billy coughed out a sudden laugh and called after him as he went down the stone staircase:

'Tell him that yourself.'

'A brazen trickster,' Tommy Martin said again as the Inspector followed Billy out on to the narrow platform which looked down on the quarry.

They watched Ward tell Blessing. A black fox-snout talking into a blonde mule's ear. They saw Blessing look away and spit. The four-wheeled draycart turned and moved toward the quarry exit.

'That fella's no laughing matter,' Quinn said to Billy as he came back into the office.

64

'I know he's a rogue,' Billy said.

'Rogues are harmless,' Quinn said, 'that fella's a villain and if it was my quarry I'd race him.'

'He's my tenant and he's behind with his rent,' Billy said, 'and if you can't work you can't pay.'

'I'd poverise him, and for good reason.'

'Can I hear why?'

Quinn looked away to where his two constables were climbing a steep path towards the top of the quarry accompaning four of Billy's workmen, each carrying two boxes of dynamite. Constable Shanley was sitting now beside the strong sealed coach.

'Can I hear why?' Billy asked again.

'No, I'm sorry, Billy, you can't,' said Quinn.

'Is it grave as that?'

'I'd mind my step with that fella . . . That's all I can tell you for now.'

Billy watched the heavy navy-blue back as Quinn descended the stone steps towards the quarry floor. Two men this morning, both allergic to Ward. A warning?

As Quinn and Shanley moved towards the sealed wagon, Ward dropped his voice and muttered, 'Up cadging a cheap tombstone from Billy Winters.' Quinn turned and almost barked:

'The cowards mutter . . . say your piece out loud, son!'

'Blessed,' Ward said aloud, 'are the peacekeepers for they shall be called the R.I.C. . . . the Queen's Royal Irish Constant Bullery!'

Shanley put his hand on his leather-covered truncheon. Quinn restrained him by saying quietly:

'Let him jape for now. When we get him in a cell some night, we'll put manners on him.'

6

At the top of the staircase, Beth paused at the hall window which looked down on the yard. From this window, twelve months ago, she had first seen Ward walk through the arched entry and stand waiting until he glanced up and saw her. Billy was away in Portland buying stone. Mercy had gone with a basket of tea, eggs, meat and bread to the hay-makers in the lake meadow beyond the fort field, a good half mile away. Beth had no idea who Ward was or what he was doing in the yard. She remembered afterwards sensing that her life would be different from that moment, would be bound up in some way with this man.

On her way down the staircase she had tried to decide who he could be: a new apprentice mason at the quarry? Some kind of merchant from Dublin or Belfast? A French or Italian mechanic for the new stone-crusher?

'Yes?' she had said at the back door.

Ward crossed the cobbles towards her. Even from where she stood she could see the cat-like tawny flecks in his green eyes. He seemed to have a slight turn in one which gave his face an uncommon look, an expression she found difficult to read. He was very good-looking, fine-skinned, dark; a kind of beardless Christ with slightly irregular teeth. His voice when he spoke was much darker than expected, a hint of Fermanagh combined with a slight American drawl:

'Is the boss about?'

'He's away till Thursday.'

'I'm Liam Ward of Brackagh.'

'Tom Ward's nephew.'

'That's me.'

'Then we're neighbours.' She held out her hand.

'I'm your father's new tenant.'

'You have a problem, Liam?'

'Yes . . . an old fool of a cow in a bog-hole and no manbody for miles about to help pull her out . . . they're all at hay.'

'We've a big pony here, you're welcome to him. Have you someone to lead him?'

And when Ward had hesitated, she said:

'I'm free: I can lead him for you.'

Very quickly he helped her to bridle and harness Punch into the gig. They were heading for Brackagh within five minutes. Sitting alongside him she was conscious of his bare arms, and because of this she had kept talking, asking one question after another which seemed embarrassing in retrospect. He had answered with ease. Only later did she realise they were skilled half-answers; he elaborated nothing. Yes, he had been gone for over ten years. Yes, he was first hired out at Clonoula as a child. Yes, he had spent a while at Florencecourt as a stable-boy. Yes, he had been six years in America, two in Dublin, and yes he had two shire horses. Today he had loaned them to a neighbour, Blinky Blessing, who had them in Enniskillen; and no, nobody could live

68

off thirty acres of Fermanagh scrubland. Or for that matter, a hundred acres of scrubland here or anywhere. The avenue of Clonoula went very steeply at the end towards the gatelodge, a track dug out of the side of an extended drumlin sometime in the eighteenth century.

Emerging onto the county road they turned sharp right, went on a hundred yards up the road, then veered left into a rutted lane between two heathery bog-mounds. Hungry scutch-grass spined the lane, tentacles of briar reaching from the verges. The whole of Brackagh as far as she could see was deep in meadowsweet, coarse wild grass and giant hemlock. Beyond this rough land, there were islands of birchwood and alder and a small lake or pond called Laban.

Above Laban Lake, Ward's house stood on a slight elevation, set in a grassy island. Half the house was thatched, the other half roofed with rusting tin. There were a few hardwood trees and a small orchard. She remembered the talk about his uncle Tom Ward: a thatcher and poacher; how he had managed to weave his way drunk up this dark lane on winter nights, year in, year out, and how everyone said he would be found in a bog-hole. In spite of the forecasts, he had died in his bed, sober.

Suddenly through the maze of cut-over bog, she saw a bovine head rear and plunge. There was a calf standing near by. The calf blared as they approached. Ward got down from the gig and led Punch towards the bog-hole. A muddy rope hung round the branch of a birch tree. She noticed a spade with a cow's horn for a handle, a black horn. He tied the rope around the cow's horns, attaching it to each side of the cob's collar. He then gave the reins to Beth:

'I'll do what I can to get her back feet up.'

He took off his shirt. Beth watched as he reached arm-deep down into the glarry ooze. He pulled up the cow's tail. He then rubbed it dry with bracken, twined it round his wrists and dug his heels into the edge of the soggy bank, nodding at Beth and saying:

'Don't give him his head ... it could break her neck.'

'I know what to do,' Beth said.

As Ward began to pull she led the cob forward very gently, keeping a backward pressure on the bit. For a moment it seemed as if nothing would happen. With a quiet gum-click she encouraged the cob to pull a little harder. The cow blared feebly. There were veins standing out on Ward's face and neck, then a suction noise as the bog slowly released its hold on the cow. It slid out like a great hunk of black liver, up the bank and on to the coarse, bluish grass. Ward kept a tension on the rope in case the cow staggered up and stumbled in again. It became very clear very quickly that the cow was too weak to move. Beth put her hand on the cow's nose; it was cold:

'She's very chilled.'

The cow was now giving great involuntary trembles every ten seconds or so. Beth had seen this before, trembles preceding coma followed by death. Ward had begun to clean off the glar and was rubbing the cow vigorously with handfuls of heather.

'Have you whiskey in the house?' Beth asked.

Ward thought about this for a moment. He then said, almost reluctantly:

'I have.'

'Tell me where and I'll get it.'

'In the dresser press, left-hand side, there's a naggin of whiskey.'

'How do I get in?'

'The water-tank at the gable: there's a stone at the corner of it, the key's under that stone.'

As she left, Ward was still rubbing the cow. She could see that it was a roan cow.

The front yard, or street, was alive with ducks, geese and hens scraping on a midden topped with scutch-grass and clumps of nettles. The tree at the gable was oak with a malignant growth half-way up and leaves that seemed luridly green. She found the key, and let herself into the kitchen. The smoke-yellowed windows were small, and the interior poorly lit. When her eyes became used to the dimness she began to see detail. It was more like a saddler's shop than the inside of a cottage: horse collars and hames, britchens and plough reins, saddles and harness, all up on holders. There was a pervasive smell of horse sweat. Everywhere she looked she saw nose-cramps, shears, dipping crooks, hay-rope makers, a clutter of familiar pastoral gadgets. A rope line across the front of the hearth was hung with three shirts, two collarless, one that looked like silk. She touched it. Silk. It was what it seemed.

On the kitchen table there were two catalogues of property sales: both London auctioneers, one of them opened and pencil-marked, coach-house inns, farms, building land. She got the whiskey from the dresser cupboard, unconsciously putting the key in her skirt pocket.

Ward was sitting apart on the root of a fallen birch. From a hundred yards or so she could tell from his posture that the cow was dead.

He got up as she approached, took the bottle and nodded his thanks. There was a silence till she asked:

'When did you see her last?'

'Yesterday sometime.'

'She could have been in there all night?'

'Very likely she was . . . she was agey.'

'It's a loss nonetheless.'

'Yes.'

He uncorked the naggin of whiskey and offered her the bottle.

'No thank you.'

She watched as he swallowed. He re-corked the bottle and said:

'I'm beholden to you, Miss.'

'I'd do the same for any neighbour.'

They looked in silence at the cow. The calf had moved away, had begun to nibble here and there through the coarse grass.

'You'll need a foster-mother.'

Ward nodded:

'There's a lot I need.'

'She could have ended worse,' Beth said.

'How?'

'In a knacker's yard.'

'What's so special about dying in a bog . . . for man or beast?'

'Don't you want to be buried with your own people?'

'When you're dead you won't know or care: no one else will either.'

'That sounds a shade . . .' she searched for a word, couldn't find one and said '. . . cold.'

'Millions of us died in the famine . . . who knows or cares now about any single one of them?'

'We all do . . . don't we?'

Ward shrugged, stood up and said:

'Miss, I'm thankful,' he said again, and began putting Punch back into the gig.

'You'll have a job burying her.'

'I'll get help later.'

She was aware as she drove away of his eyes on her back. She knew also that she would not mention this episode to Mercy Boyle, nor to Billy when he returned.

Half-way up the avenue in the failing light she remembered the key in her pocket. Should she go back now or wait till morning? He might be forced to break a window or the lock. He was probably still in the bog burying the cow. She turned the gig and headed back down the avenue again. It was almost dark now in the lane that led to Brackagh. Approaching the area where the cow had died, she saw Ward walking towards the lane-way carrying a spade. In the distance she could see another spade-man topping up the cow's grave. She reined the pony, waiting till she could make out his face:

'I put your key in my pocket and forgot. I'm sorry.'

As she was feeling for the key she said:

'I can bring you home if you like.'

'I'll not say no to that,' Ward said.

'You got help burying her.'

'Your other tenant, Blinky Blessing.'

'You must be exhausted.'

'I wouldn't be on for a jig at the minute.'

She heard herself laugh:

'I'm sorry.'

'For what?' Ward said. 'You've had all the bother.'

At the door of the cottage he said:

'I can give you tea with no milk.'

She heard herself say:

'I take it that way.'

She sat on a creepie under the chimney and watched him rake back the greesach of hot embers, handing him kindling of small turf and twigs, heather from under the creepie. He scooped up water with a white enamel bucket from a tub in the corner, filled a black kettle and swung it over the fire. He then placed two brown eggs in a blackened pot and placed them to boil against the burning turf. When he went down the room towards a wide shelf stacked with bags, jars and tins, she heard a soft flop-noise, and saw then with horror the blind scurry of a rat towards the kitchen door. From where he stood Ward gave a sudden jump, landing with both feet on the rat: crushing it under his boots. To stop it twitching he dug the heel of his studded boot across its neck. He then opened the door and kicked the rat out to the dark street. She felt slightly sick. He went back to the shelf, opened a square tin and took out a loaf of shop bread:

'That fair sickened you, I'd say?'

'A little.'

'Bad cess to them; they can eat their way through stone walls.'

'Don't you have a cat?'

'It died.'

'We've a dozen yard-cats, half-wild; no rats get near the house . . . take two if you can catch them.'

He pushed the brochures, catalogues and newspapers to one side, brushed the board table with his forearm and placed two mugs on it. Inside, the mugs were so brown she could scarcely see the tea when it was poured. She said 'No thank you' to the sugar, watching him put four heaped spoonfuls into his mug before buttering thick slices of bread which he had with the boiled eggs. He ate very quickly, swallowing mouthfuls of

74

the hot, sweet tea. He pointed at the loaf with his knife, offering.

'No thank you,' she said picking up a brochure:

'Is this private?'

He shook his head. She began to read the advertisements underlined in pencil. It had to do with steam passage to America and Canada, grants of land in Canada.

'Are you planning to emigrate?'

'It's a neighbour man marked those . . . I'd be more for the Yukon or South Africa . . . Gold.'

'Don't you care about Brackagh?'

Ward shook his head.

'Growing up,' Beth said, 'I used to think this bog and Laban Lake were strange and beautiful. A kind of paradise.'

'Try living here. You'd have the same life as that rat; and who'd choose to slave and be beggared in a bog?'

'Mr Parnell's changing all that.'

'He can't change the weather, stop blight or beggary, and he's no King to me . . .'

He smiled through misshapen teeth. In the candlelight she could see clearly the whin fleck in his greeny eyes and the slight squint in his left eye. A hint of tinker? Of mongrel treachery? Sipping the strong black tea, she could not decide if the face was gentle or brutal, cunning or innocent, or a blend of all these.

'This was your uncle's house?'

Ward nodded.

'Where are your parents?'

'The mother's in Blaney workhouse.'

'I'm sorry.'

He tapped his forehead with a forefinger.

'She doesn't know anyone this brave while.'

'Brothers? Sisters?'

Ward shook his head and muttered 'None'.

'And your father?'

'When I was twelve, he walked out one night for good or bad . . . He never came back.'

He continued eating, buttering more bread, sprinkling it with sugar, refilling his mug with tea. He stood suddenly, lit a storm lantern and placed it on the table. The lantern illuminated more detail than she had noticed earlier, the familiar clutter hanging from the chimney breast: snaffles, nose-tongs, gaffs, thatching needles and other gadgetry, some of it unfamiliar.

Resting directly on the mantelpiece were two prints, one of the Sacred Heart, the other a graphic version of the terrified sinner being dragged from bed by horned smiling devils with reptilian eyes, cloven feet and long tails. She could sense Ward's eyes on her back. Expecting comment she waited. Silence, till she was forced to ask:

'Are you Catholic?'

'What else could I be?'

He thumbed up at the two prints on the mantelpiece:

'The long-tailed lads look to be more fun than the boy with the showy heart.'

She was surprised by both the casual blasphemy and the sound of her own laughter which seemed to reverberate around the high ceiling-boards. He smiled oddly, watching her.

It was black dark when he led Punch down the hazardous lane to the country road, where again he thanked her with the same, odd formality. For days, weeks afterwards, she found herself going over and over every detail of that first meeting.

It was mid-November, All Souls, when she saw him again. She was standing at her mother's grave, which was isolated in an older area of the graveyard dominated by four very tall yew trees; one dead.

A disembodied voice seemed to come from behind the dead yew. She then realised with a sudden heart-jerk that it was Ward's voice. He came over, capless in a black Crombie coat which looked two sizes too big, a black-and-white check neck-scarf and fine black boots. The effect, she thought, was a cross between a bookmaker and a country undertaker. Images of a dream she had earlier that morning had been recurring all day, and as he approached now it was almost as though he could read her thoughts. Then she heard herself say:

'Do you have family buried here?'

'No ... but I guessed you'd come and I know Billy's away.'

She nodded, as Ward said:

'Maybe we could meet later?'

Silence for a minute until she asked:

'How? ... Where?'

'Brackagh.'

'I couldn't travel that lane in the dark.'

'I'll be on the county road.'

She had been forced to lie to Mercy about posting a letter in the village.

'It won't go till tomorrow, Miss, you might as well wait till daylight.'

'I'd like the walk.'

'I'll come with you so.'

'No, no, Mercy, why should you ... I'm not afraid of the dark.'

And it was dark on the avenue and she was a little

afraid. Gradually she began to see detail: railings, the verge, the gleam of pot-holes, lighted gaps to the west through the blackness of laurel and trees.

The footpath through the scrub was glarry in places. It stuck to her boots, scraggy November briars dragging at her skirt and coat as her heart began to throb unevenly. About half-way down the path she could see across to Brackagh and the light of a paraffin lamp shining through the window of Ward's cottage.

She hesitated. He would be down there at his lane-entry on the county road waiting to escort her. What then? What do I know about him? Almost nothing. Am I being deeply stupid? No. I must get to know him better; that's why I'm doing this, to get to know him better, isn't it? Do I love him? He's seldom far from my thoughts. And is that love? Fascinates me certainly. Do I even like him? Could be I more dislike than like . . . The false urbanity, the acquired drawl, the shrug, the dusty views, the strange courtesy more a barrier than true kindness; and he hates this landscape I love so much. Vain too . . . ambitious to be something else, to be someone else, to be somewhere else . . . all a first impression . . . Yes I must get to know him better, that's why I'm going, isn't it?

Ten yards further on she heard a voice in her head say 'Don't pretend you fool,' and again the vividness of an early-morning dream came back, Ward's hand up Mercy Boyle's skirt and Mercy moaning, 'God, I'm dying for it, Liam, come on,' and while he was thrusting at Mercy she could feel his other hand pleasuring between her own thighs.

All that morning she had been tempted to question Mercy about Ward. She could find no way. She kept repeating to herself, 'a dream is a dream is a dream . . .

it's nothing'; and the more she told herself it was nothing the more it seemed like something.

She stopped. What am I afraid of? Intimacy? No. Of being discovered by Billy Winters? Banished from Clonoula? Yes, I certainly fear that. Why then had she said 'Yes' in the graveyard this afternoon?

Down somewhere ahead of her on the road, Ward was waiting in the dark. She remembered now the sudden jump and the rat death, and the effect of the greasy floor, the farm- and fish-tackle on the wall, the smoke-yellowed famine windows, the dying sinner, the Sacred Heart; no place for a tryst.

She turned, went back to the avenue, down to the post office where she posted a letter, bought a bag of groceries and returned to her bedroom where she wrote:

Clonoula,
All Souls, 1882

Dear Liam,
Just now, from the avenue planting,
I saw the light in your kitchen and could not
go on. I am not sure why, unless it be that
I'm blessed or cursed with an uncommon
amount of common sense which tells me that
secret meetings are silly and must soon be
discovered. Open association would cause
outrage here. B.W. has described you now
and then with unkind words. That does not
worry me overmuch. I could describe him with
unkinder ones.
I am sorry to have left you standing down there
in the dark. I feel now I should have gone on.

*How otherwise can I ascertain the many things I
want to know about you?*

*What I am certain of is that you are seldom far
from my mind and heart.*

*Be patient as I must be. We'll meet soon.
Meantime you have my apologies . . . next time
I'll keep my word.*

Elizabeth

The following morning she tore up the letter. Katie
Carroll in the post office would have it steamed, read
and closed again in ten minutes.

Weeks passed: then months. Ward was gone, no one
knew where for certain. Dublin? Glasgow? London?
'Oh, some roguery,' Billy said; 'the like of that fellow could be married over there with a house full of
children.'

It was almost midsummer when Ward led Punch
into the cobbled yard. He stood patting his neck talking
quietly. There was sweat over its entire body. Beth was
so startled to see him she was on the edge of trembling
herself:

'Where was he?' she had asked.

'Comin' down the road hell for leather.'

'Something must have frightened him.'

'Horse-flies most likely . . . he'll be all right.'

'And where were you all this while?'

'That's a long story.'

He had led Punch into the stable and began to wipe
him down. She had carried water from the cistern, meal
from the bin, and within minutes it was established
that Billy Winters was up at Annalong buying granite.

He'd be gone a few days. They arranged to meet at the lough-side where the upside-down curragh was, before dawn on Friday the second of June.

She had left a note on the kitchen table for Mercy; a lie. This troubled her. There was the likelihood that she could be seen by other lovers, by a beggar in the half-light of a midsummer's dawn. She would have to go up the house-field ditch, and through the fort, then over to the ravine. Once down in the greeny-brown underwater gloom of the ravine floor, it was almost two miles following the rivulet to the shore of the lough, an unlikely place to encounter anything but otter, fox, rabbit, badger or squirrel. But there could be someone fishing on the lough as dawn neared. It was the foolishness, the risk that was so attractive, the longing to be reckless for a day or two, a time out of humdrum, a feasting on sin and senses.

Can't I advise myself, she thought. Am I lovelorn? Foolish? Fascinated? A moth to the candle? A rabbit in hawk-shadow? My heart ripped out for a dog to tear?

She dressed and left her bedroom, avoiding the creaking board in the upper landing, the door with the tell-tale hinges in the lower hall. Then the kitchen. Silence, but for the wall-clock.

She wrote on the back of a used envelope in pencil:

Dear Mercy,
1.30 a.m. Tuesday.
Message by hand just now from a troubled
friend.
Back tomorrow night or Saturday at latest.
Work-list on dresser.
Don't let men bully you.

She signed it: *Beth*.

And then scribbled a P.S.:

Mince leftover mutton for today's dinner.
Key of pantry and cellar in drawer of sewing
machine.
Get Mickey to help you churn.
Keep back door locked.
Others have no business in kitchen or house apart
from mealtime.
If Corranny cow calves, keep beistings.
If nervous at night, get your sister Etta to stay.

Wrapped in newspaper, she took brown bread, butter, a small jar of milk, sugar, a portion of smoked bacon and tea, and put them in a canvas bag. When the dawn coolness met her outside she went back to the basement hall and put on a rainproof jacket. She then left from the yard by going through the kitchen garden and from there into the haggard. Then up by the house-field ditch to the fort field, all the time keeping out of sight of the house. Nothing but the sound of cattle cudding under trees, the occasional bleat of lamb or ewe, the sudden flurry of pigeons in the pine-tops round the fort.

She went through the fort towards the ravine, a black cleft in the brightening landscape. It was just gone three o'clock. The two hundred feet of path to the rivulet led down, she knew, at a broken thornbush. Twice branches caught at her dress, the second time unstitching the front seam. When her foot caught in the bare forked roots of ash, they grazed her ankle. It became darker as she went lower, fern fronds growing evilly from the mossy branches of elongated oak. Utter silence and solitude as she reached the floor of the ravine with its grave-wide rivulet, its bed of rust-iron stones under brown pools flecked with amber foam.

At first she thought it was the cry of a vixen calling her cubs. No? Behind, ahead, above? It seemed to be approaching, a creature in distress ... bird or beast ... There it was again, closer, almost human-sounding. Flying? Running? Could it be ... an infant cry? She felt the creep of horror at the nape of her neck as she strained, trying to see. The squealing seemed alongside her. Then she saw it ... a white owl grounded, a baby rabbit gripped in his talons, the hooked beak tearing ravenously into the wriggling upturned stomach. Suddenly her voice blended with the rabbit squeals as she stumbled towards them crying out.

The owl backflapped into flight, still gripping its prey, until it gained enough height to circle and glide away toward the lough, down the dark winding rivulet, the rabbit squeals growing fainter and fainter, the cries so human she felt tears smarting in her eyes.

She took off her left shoe and stocking. The knuckle of her ankle looked bruised. Sitting on a dry stone, she immersed it in a pool. The water was soothing. She then watched it dry on another stone as a faint throbbing pain returned. From the pocket of her riding jacket she took a small penknife, cut a thornbush and used a few thorns to close the torn seam of her dress. Away high above Tyrone the sun had risen, light now filtering down into Fermanagh; down into the ravine, sharpening the undertones of grass, leaf, bark and moss, fern and water.

She began walking, crossing and re-crossing the rivulet dozens of times to avoid tentacles of briar and clumps of tall anaemic nettles. For the last quarter of a mile the height diminished with every step, until gradually the landscape opened on either side to fields sloping towards the shore of the Lower Lough. She had been concentrating so much on her footing that she was startled to see Ward sitting on the side of the curragh, staring out at the water. Instinctively she stepped behind a screen of alder as she thought, What am I doing here! I must be mad.

Through the alder, she watched Ward roll and light a cigarette, muttering to herself, 'What's wrong with you. Don't be silly.' She began walking towards the shore.

Hearing her come, Ward pushed the tarred coracle half into the water and said:

'You hurt your ankle?'

'Am I limping?'

'Just what you'd remark.'

'I caught it coming down.'

'It's tricky enough in daylight.'

'You must know it well.'

'I do.'

He pointed to a seat in the back of the boat. When she was sitting, he took off his boots and stockings, rolled up his trousers and pushed the curragh clear of the stony shore. As it floated out into deep water she could feel him easing his body into a kneeling position behind her. She then felt both his hands on her shoulders. As he steadied both the balance of his body and the curragh, she turned to say, 'Am I in your way?' and was surprised by the alarm in his voice as he shouted: 'Keep still!'

She kept very still, holding both sides. It steadied. He clambered past her very carefully and sat on the middle board. He then began pulling out the oars and fixing them into the oarlocks, and although he smiled she could see that he was tense and he seemed unnatural.

'I'm sorry, Liam . . . did I frighten you?'

'These things cope very handy.'

'That'd be a silly start to the day.'

'Or a bad end,' Ward said, 'I don't swim.'

'I do,' she said, 'I'd save you!'

He began to row over a membrane of grey stillness, miles and miles of water. High above them the hysteria of early feeding swallows sounded faintly and seemed as small as the insects they were feeding on.

'Dear God, it's quiet . . . look.'

Ward nodded.

'Is that bad for fishing?'

He nodded towards a pattern of circles fifty yards away.

'They're feeding . . . that's good.'

He shipped the oars, took an otter-board from the floor of the cot, and placed it in the water. She could see fly-lines with dozens of coloured flies attached to the board. Ward was ensuring they were not tangled. Satisfied, he aimed the otter-board towards the feeding trout giving it a small push to get it moving. It seemed to propel itself sideways towards the feeding trout. She could see why it was called 'an otter' – dipping and wriggling slightly as it moved through the water. Fascinated, she watched as it passed to the left of the feeding circles. It up-ended, and disappeared for a moment, as the water became suddenly alive with trout pulsing and flashing as they tried to disengage from the barbed hooks.

Ward balled the slack, pulling the board back toward the curragh with a circular hand-movement. It reminded her of a woman spinning wool. She could see from the tension on the line that the hooked fish had remained hooked. In less than two minutes there were five trout, two of them a good size, flipping, somersaulting on the floor of the cot. He pointed at her feet and said:

'Under your seat . . . the priest.'

'The what?'

'It's a gaff . . . and *don't stand*,' he said with an odd grimace.

She leaned forward, groping under the seat. Her hand closed on something steel, a blacksmith-made gaff with a hooked head. Ward held each fish and dispatched it with an accurate blow to the skull. He then unhooked the trout, tidied up the tangled fly-lines and main-line, and placed the otter-board between two wooden ribs of the cot. She could sense that he was very pleased with himself.

'Is it as easy as it looks?'

'Less or more.'

'And can you catch them like that every time?'

'Less or more.'

'Which is it, less or more?'

'It's more slaughter than sport . . . It's not legal.' He was rowing again. For a man so narrowly built, he seemed strong, the cot gliding over the surface so smoothly that she scarcely noticed the pull of the oars as they plunged and surfaced in a dripping arc, entering and re-entering almost soundlessly.

In little over half an hour, they had reached the natural jetty at Corvey Island. Ward pushed the cot under a tunnel of overhanging alder and thorn, tied it to a root and climbed up the steep bank on to the island.

She had gone ahead to the bothy, a single-roomed herd's cabin. When she was a child she could remember tin being ferried over to avoid the nuisance of thatching. Inside there was an open hearth with a swinging pot-holder, one table, two chairs, a settle bed with a straw mattress, two windows with board shutters on the inside, one dresser scarce of Delft, its lower cupboard containing pots, pans, basins and buckets.

Through the open door she could see the sun shining on a crag at the water's edge. On the crag a cormorant perched very still, its wings tensed for flight. There was a surface spring-well a hundred yards from the bothy. When she returned with an enamel bucket full of water, Ward had the fire going and was gutting the trout. She fried the fish and they ate them at the board table with bread and butter. Then they drank tea and talked until midday and beyond. At one stage Ward, looking out at the lake, had asked or said:

'This is all Billy Winters'.'

'No,' she'd said, 'my mother promised me this when I was four. Billy put cattle on it once and then complained it wasn't worth the trouble. My mother said Cuchulain summered here, drinking mead and setting snares for deer, and out from the island there were nets and ropes to the kitchen window and a bell on every rope, to ring out a run of salmon.'

'That's handier than an otter-board . . . A body could live well here.'

'Paradise must have been something like this.'

'Billy Winters could double well enough for a God . . . of sorts.'

'Why don't you like him?'

'Why don't you?'

'I asked first.'

'He's the breed of landlord: they're all the one, that class: bad.'

For ten minutes she had found herself defending Billy Winters and pointing out that Parnell was a landlord. Ward would have none of it.

'Why do you talk and think like no one hereabouts?'

'I've been away a long time.'

'When you were hired here as a child, what were you put to?'

'Pickin' spuds, gathering stones.'

'Then what?'

'Florencecourt, the Earl of Enniskillen. That's where I got to know about horses. He swapped me with Lord Erne for a Scottish butler. Erne sent me over to his place in Mayo; run by his agent, Boycott.'

'You worked with Captain Boycott?'

'Under . . . not for long, slave, slave, slave till you drop. He had a system of fines . . . if you hummed of whiskey from the night before, he'd smell your breath and you'd be fined as "unfit". He'd fine you for being a minute late, for losing or breaking a spade or a billhook. Some of the lads ended up *owing* money at the end of the week! Didn't suit the Mayo men one bit.'

'Then where?'

'America . . . for six years, Boston mostly, and New York, then back to Dublin for a few years, then the uncle here died and left me Brackagh and four years' unpaid rent.'

'And what were you doing in Dublin?'

'The aunt had properties . . . I minded them.'

'You collected rent, Liam.'

'I fixed doors, slates, floors, gathered the odd shilling.'

She had laughed and repeated: 'You collected rent . . . You've been a rent collector like the people you profess to hate, so tell me again why you hate Billy Winters?'

'Did I say I hated him?'

'Something very like.'

'I said he was of the hated class . . . landlords . . . and they're all alike . . . criminals.'

88

'Tell me Billy's crimes, the ones I don't know about, because I know he doesn't cane *you* for rent or Blessing or Ruttledge or anyone else.'

Ward looked impassively at the clay floor for quite a while, then out at the glittering water. For a minute she thought he was not going to elaborate till she heard him say quietly:

'They say he works for the Castle.'

At first she did not understand. When she did, she began to laugh, awkwardly, unnaturally. Ward turned to look at her, his face immobile as she said:

'A spy! An informer! I've never heard such silliness!'

'Why is that?'

'Spying on neighbours for money! He doesn't need that sort of money.'

'He might do it for nothing, for loyalty, for the Crown, for Ulster, for the Union, to keep the grip on us ... all gentry are ready-made spies, everyone knows that.'

'You're not joking ... are you?'

'No, he's been to the Castle twice this last while, Billy Winters, his twin or his double ... so they say.'

She thought about this for a moment.

'How could you know such a thing? Who are "they"?'

'Talk.'

'Then you must *talk* with people who *talk* that way about Billy Winters ... Fenians, are they? Are you?'

'Everyone here talks that way.'

'I know he goes to the Castle for import licences, for Italian marble, for Swedish dynamite, for German spare parts; it's all business, all very strict ... informing is not one of his crimes.'

'He has others?'

When she did not answer Ward took out a gold

pocket-watch, and pressed it open. She saw that it was almost two o'clock. He left the watch on the table and then doused the burning turf with a wet hessian bag.

'Why are you doing that?'

'The "Coolmore" passes here at three every day, comes back at six . . . we can light it again later.'

As she reached for the pocket-watch she asked:

'May I look?'

She pressed the spring clip. An elegant white face with black Roman numerals. Inscribed on the inside of the gold cover she read:

For my darling Stewart
This timepiece is
For all time
Love from Susan
Christmas 1828

'Oh dear,' she muttered, 'poor Susan, poor Stewart.'

'It's American,' Ward said.

'Who were they?'

Ward shrugged.

'I won it at poker.'

'I thought maybe it was your mother and father's.'

Ward gave a quick short laugh.

'Stewart! . . . Susan? . . . Packie and Mary Josephine; Packie Ward from Aughaward, where we mattered once, long ago before the Stewarts and the Billys and the Gilberts and the Cecils took it from us.'

'We still matter.'

'With nothing? You count for nothing.'

'Things don't matter, Liam.'

'Easy said when you're reared at Clonoula. You talked early on about men sitting half the day in the kitchen with cows half-milked, pigs not cleaned out, everything half-done throughother, a mess ... that's because of "things", because it's part yours.'

'Nothing's mine at Clonoula nor likely to be.'

'You're his only kin.'

She paused and looked at him steadily:

'You know I'm not.'

'Is that not talk?'

She shook her head.

'And you're certain sure?'

'Since I was twelve.'

'And does *he* know *you* know?'

'It came out once when he was drunk. Next day he let on he couldn't remember, but he knows I know. I think sometimes he hates me. Oftentimes I hate him so much ... I could kill him. If I could ... kill him.'

'You're having me on.'

She shook her head.

'Is he worth hanging for?'

Ward took out tobacco and cigarette papers, rolled and lit a cigarette before asking:

'Why would you take on to murder him?'

'Kill I said ... not murder.'

'Is there a difference?'

'I couldn't plan it ... anyway, when I'm not hating him I sometimes think I maybe love him: in a way.'

'"Oftentimes," you said.'

'Once I heard him hit my mother ... I was very small. From that night out, I feared and loathed him and wished him dead ... I still do.'

'For hitting her?'

'And for what I didn't understand at first. When he'd kiss me not fatherly, I couldn't tell my mother. Maybe she guessed ... I think he did it to make her

91

unhappy . . . for revenge, and he should answer for that . . . That's what I felt at her burial, and ever since.'

'Black thoughts,' Ward muttered.

'Don't you have them about some things?'

Ward turned, looked into her eyes and smiled in a way that she would remember afterwards with extraordinary vividness. He stood and walked to the doorway. A mile away across the placid water, the heavy thrum of a marine engine driving the 'Coolmore' paddle-steamer reached them, muted by the distance.

'We should go out a while.'

There was a map of Corvey Island hanging in her bedroom. As a child it had fascinated her with its graphics of goat and cormorant, trout and curlew. There was a compass sign, at the top, a lined reference on the right-hand side giving acreage, description and detail: bog, rock, wood, lough-shore, well, garden. The total acreage was thirty acres, two roods and three perches. The 'garden' was a small circle of rich soil behind and below the bothy, protected on all sides by rock, whin and thornbush. They walked through its cushioned greenness and up a steep path to a clear view of the island, lough and landscape beyond.

The 'Coolmore' was well on its way to Ballyshannon, exhaust plumes in the air, the corrugations on the water levelling, the faraway heartbeat of the engine dying away into an absolute silence. Through that afternoon silence and well into evening, they made love as naturally as they had eaten and talked earlier, though she was conscious later that she had eaten more hungrily, talked more openly and made love more passionately than he. It was dark when the 'Coolmore' passed, going back to Enniskillen.

In the bothy the fire was re-lit, the settle-bed opened

and what seemed like an embarrassment was accomplished without awkwardness. The mattress was placed on its side before the fire, the bed linen and blankets strung up like love emblems on a string from wall to wall. The door was closed and candles lit against the dark, and they ate again, the cheese and bacon sandwiches she had brought. He persuaded her to try hot whiskey with sugar, which she did, and they placed the mattress on the floor, made love and watched the fire, half-talking, half-sleeping. Every now and then Ward kept returning to what they had talked about earlier. Had she ever, he asked, wondered about her true father? 'My untrue father. Every other day and often in dreams.' In one dream, she said, he was a young boy washed out to sea and drowned and oh the grief of it and yet she felt her father must be heartless, a betrayer or liar, or already married perhaps; weak, unkind; and that her mother, if you thought about it, had been foolish as a girl, dishonest to marry carrying another's child, and you could understand Billy but not forgive . . . Blame on both sides. After a long silence, Ward asked:

'Has he quit?'

'What are you asking me?'

'Interfering.'

'Only when he's drunk . . . It's more silly than frightening.'

She then told him about the night of the safe, the beaver hat, the drawer of gold, and how he pretended to have forgotten all about it the following day. She could tell that Ward was listening very intently. When she stopped talking, he lay very still for some minutes and suddenly got up on his elbow to look at her in the light of the fire.

'Gold? How much is there?'

93

'A steel drawer full; the bottom of the safe.'

'What would that weigh?'

'I don't know . . . a lot I'd say.'

Ward whistled quietly, lay back and asked:

'How long is it there?'

'Before Napoleon's time . . . a hundred years.'

'Empire loot,' Ward said, 'the stuff that makes Winchesters to shoot Indians and Africans,' and then he added, after a moment, '. . . and us.'

When she awoke, Ward was asleep. She went to the door and looked out. The sun was gold on the grass of the enclosed garden, on the whins and thorns above and on the lough below a blinding of silver. When she went down to wash in a baylet, a fish belly-jumped far out. The surface flashed like diamonds and it seemed to her that nobody in the round world could be as completely alive and happy as she felt at that moment.

In the bothy Ward was still stretched on the mattress, his eyes closed though she could tell that he was awake. She was startled when he spoke:

'Killing is a small thing . . . Getting away with it . . . that's not easy.'

Was he lying there planning to murder Billy Winters or was he clowning or half in earnest:

'What are you saying Liam?'

He got up on his elbow and looked over and said:

'Why not take what we need . . . what he doesn't need? What's locked away a hundred years . . . the ill-gotten gold.'

The bothy was so quiet she could hear the faraway fluting of a curlew. When it stopped she knew she was blinking unnaturally and was surprised when she heard herself say:

'How?'

'I've bromides can pacify a nervous horse; they'd put a man asleep for two days . . . Some of that in his nightcap and we'll be in Dublin or Belfast before he'd waken.'

She could see the excitement in his face: gold more real to him than love, honour, beauty or truth. It could buy anything in the world but the spirit of Christ. She understood his excitement all too well. Since that night, the image of fistfuls of gold had recurred over and over again. Like Ward she had thought of different ways it could be taken with absolute safety. With every scheme there were two or three impossibilities. Ward's suggestion now was so simple, so cunning that she found herself looking at his face, trying to read behind it into his mind and heart:

'And if we're caught?'

'We can't think of that.'

'And do I just walk out of the house where I was born and grew up, and where my mother died, away from Billy Winters – forever?'

'You said you'd be glad to.'

'In one way; another way it'd be a kind of death.'

Ward thought about this for a while before smiling oddly and saying:

'If what the clergy teach is true, *that* can be a beginning of sorts.'

'You've an answer for everything, Liam!'

'Almost,' Ward said.

7

Billy Winters was eating a bacon sandwich and checking sandstone lengths when he heard Tommy Martin shout through the noise of the crusher. Tommy was pointing towards the quarry entrance:

'Boss, a gentleman for you here.'

Billy Winters turned and saw Kinsella's hired gig in the quarry. A young man dressed more for city than country had just stepped down. He was carrying a valise and listening as the cabby pointed up the stone staircase leading to the quarry office. He then pointed at Billy Winters. The young man then had a further word with the cabby, asking him to wait before moving across the quarry floor, picking his steps between cart-ruts and pot-holes averting his head from the pervasive crusher dust. He had a longish face, beech-hued hair and pale eyes and spoke first, holding out his free hand; an English voice; regional:

'Mr Winters?'

'That's me,' Billy said.

'Maurice Fairbrother; are you free to talk a little?'

As they moved towards the staircase leading to the quarry office Billy Winters asked:

'Are you buying or selling, Mr Fairbrother?'

'Enquiring.'

'I'll answer as best I can . . . You go on up, tell Tommy Martin up there I want a word with him down here . . . I'll be with you in five minutes.'

Maurice Fairbrother went lightly up the stone staircase to the quarry office and gave Billy's message to Tommy Martin. A wall-clock ticked behind a cluttered desk. It said half-past four. A window looked down on the monumental works, the lower lough and its islands. He could see Billy Winters walking and talking with Tommy Martin and two policemen.

Last night, in the dining-room of the Westenra Arms Hotel in Monaghan Town, he had been sitting with an American couple and three commercial travellers. The dining-room was quiet. They could hear a noisy hubbub coming from the public bar, voices angry about 'grippers', process-servers, agents, Parnell and landlords, all of it so familiar that he listened without hearing until a voice louder than the rest shouted: 'Poor Lord Frederick! Yis are a pack of hypocrites. Wasn't he a Duke's son from a palace in England, and where did they get what they got? Where did Shirley down the road get sixty-seven thousand acres of *our land*. From the crooked crown! from that old whore Elizabeth! And what have they ever give us? The workhouse, torture, rack-rents, starvation, coffin ships, the graveyard . . . Poor Lord Frederick my arse! I'll shed no tears for poor Lord Frederick or any English Lord . . . I'd cut the fuckers' throats, every last one of them, and that wouldn't half pay for what they done to us, and still do if they were let . . . Mister Parnell's right! . . . get shot of them now, forever!'

When he saw the Americans half-smiling, half-anxious,

he left the dining-room, went up to his bedroom, and opened the details copied from Mallon's file. He read again the cryptic sentences:

'Ward, Liam (32), listed I.R.B. Dublin, London and Boston branches. Helped smuggle surgical knives that murdered Lord Frederick Cavendish. The informant James Carey his uncle-in-law. Addiction to gambling. Absconded with I.R.B. funds (Dublin). Says very little. Reckoned cunning and cold. Tynan described him as "a conniving rat". Threatened with death if funds not returned. Presently lying low on uncle's small farm at Brackagh, part of Clonoula Estate, Co. Fermanagh. Tenant of William Hudson Winters. Keep on a long rein.'

Winters, William Hudson (49), Clonoula, Co. Fermanagh. Petty landlord. Church of Ireland. Old-fashioned Butt-type Unionist. Not a member of the Land League. Parnell stayed with him Feb. '83. Prone to drinking bouts. Fluent Irish. Attends Catholic funerals. Station masses at the house. Widower. Employees and tenants half R.C., half Protestant. Only daughter R.C. Well got with Catholic and dissenting clergy. Married Catherine Maguire (R.C.) deceased. Complaint to R.I.C. Enniskillen (1869) that he beat her drunkenly and once locked her out. Complaint withdrawn two days later. A maidservant (Mercy Boyle) says he molests his only daughter, Elizabeth. Incipient incest? Ward has spent a night with her in a shack on Corvey Island. Also at least two other protracted night *assignations. Winters ignorant of this. A kite worth flying?'*

Mallon had put his bony forefinger on the word 'incest' and said:

'There's your lever . . . if you care to use it.'

'How?'

'I've no notion. Throw it out – more as a hint than accusation – he might nibble, if guilty.'

As Billy came in the office door Maurice Fairbrother turned from the window:

'I'd no idea Fermanagh was so beautiful.'

'Its all the water,' Billy said, 'and the light in the water, and on the water. Fair Fermanagh: no place on earth quite like it.'

Fairbrother nodded towards a door behind Billy's desk and asked:

'Are we alone here?'

'At the minute . . . yes.'

There was quite a pause.

'I'll not waste your time, Mr Winters. My brief here has to do with Lord Frederick's murder.'

'I thought the heroes who did that were hung, all but young Brady?'

'We need more detail. The knives, as you know, were smuggled by a Mrs Byrne and procured by a Dr Hamilton Williams from Weiss of Bond Street. She had an accomplice, we suspect he is both neighbour and tenant of yours . . . man called Ward . . . Liam Ward.'

Billy was staring at the floor. He glanced up as Fairbrother said:

'You must know him, Sir?'

'He was in this room a few hours ago. Is he one of them? An "invincible"?'

'He knows them well enough to steal their funds.'

'Dear God,' Billy muttered, almost inaudibly.

'Inspector Mallon has him on a long rein; he's been watched this last year very closely.'

Maurice Fairbrother hesitated, looked up at the wall-clock and then straight into Billy's eyes, where cold pewter met a hard gravel stare:

'As I've said we need more information, Sir.'

'I can't help: I know nothing.'

'But you will if you can, Mr Winters?'

'How? if I know nothing?'

'You're a benign landowner, you're congenial with both sides, a successful businessman and, as a Unionist, you would, I presume, lean toward a progressive view of a pacific world under the Crown?'

'You presume too much, Sir.'

'Is Mr Parnell your guiding light?'

'Where did you get this stuff about me?'

'Common sense. You're like a million other Ulster men.'

'Am I?'

'Look, we're not talking about backstreet cut-throats, we're talking about the evil that guides them: the cells in Dublin, Boston, Glasgow, Birmingham, Sydney, Paris and God knows where else. We're talking about hatred versus loyalty to progress and a benign democratic Empire, we're talking about improving the lot of man-kind here and elsewhere . . . with God's help, and with yours.'

Billy shrugged and shifted uneasily.

'No, I think you *can* help, Mr Winters . . . and I believe you *should*.'

Billy Winters looked away to the dusty window. How could this man utter such stuff with a straight face? Does he believe it? The big battalions of the blessed plot? ruling half the world. He presumes too much, presumes I'll tell him something. Why me?

'As you can see I have a quarry here,' Billy said, 'a stone-cutting business. My cows milk, my dovecotes are full, my hens lay, my cattle and pigs fatten, my garden yields, there's an orchard full of Bramleys, I have ditches growing timber and bogs full of turf, and when the rain rains the grass grows, and when it shines we make hay or cut corn, and so on it goes from Lammas to Lammas. I believe in that, Mr Fairbrother, and in damn little else, and I'm not over-fond of informers.'

'No one is.'

'Most other men would by now have shown you the door; some would have kicked you down the stairs.'

'I daresay you're right . . . you haven't.'

Billy pointed at the door:

'There's the door, Mr Fairbrother; I think you should make for it.'

Maurice Fairbrother did not move for about half a minute. He then got up and stood beside the window, put his valise on Tommy Martin's high desk, unstrapped it and took out a carbon copy of notes and placed them in front of Billy Winters.

'What's this?' Billy asked, feeling about his jacket pocket for spectacles, half-looking round the top of his desk, half-glancing at the blurred words on the sheet of paper as Fairbrother said:

'It's the copy of a complaint lodged by your late wife Catherine at Enniskillen barracks fourteen years ago. She withdrew it the following day. You must know what it's about. Police reports tend to use words like "molest". I looked it up. It means interfere harmfully, to cause acute distress, to abuse, to brutalise, to debase.'

Fairbrother paused. He could see a tremor in Billy Winters' hands. Glancing up he saw the fresh face had become like a death mask.

'I tell you this only because I think you should know what's happening in your own house, to be forewarned.'

'Of what?'

'You have an island in the lower lake.'

'Corvey Island, my wife's . . . now my daughter's.'

Behind the masonry shed a hand-siren began to wind. The whining noise rising gradually to a steady howl. As it began to lessen Maurice Fairbrother went to the window and looked down.

'To be forewarned of what?' Billy asked.

Fairbrother ignored the question.

Quarry workers and police were now walking towards the quarry exit. Fairbrother watched till they were out of sight:

'You have a foreman down there; would he, for example, know or suspect anything about missing dynamite?'

Billy Winters did not reply. Maurice Fairbrother waited at the window for over a minute before speaking:

'You have six tenements in the village, the post office-cum-grocery and two cabins on your land.'

Fairbrother paused again, looking for the words he had rehearsed; found them:

'Are you saying from all these people there's none can tell you anything, none in your debt who can oblige a query?'

'What could poor folk know about a man like Ward?'

'A great deal if you ventured to ask.'

Billy Winters' breathing became visibly affected, causing his voice to wobble angrily, oddly:

'You're in the wrong shop, Sir, and your tell-tale foolscap can't dock me for old sorrows.'

'What I'm asking is simple, from someone we presumed loyal.'

He moved from the window, suddenly lifting the sheet of paper from Billy Winters' desk. He replaced it in the valise, saying as he closed it:

'She "knows" him.'

The silence that followed forced Billy Winters to ask:

'What are you saying now?'

'I've just said it. She "knows" him.'

'Talk plain, Sir.'

'Your daughter spent a night with Ward in a shack on Corvey Island. Is that plain enough? Also there were at least two protracted "assignations" in the woodland that flanks your avenue. That's what the report says: "assignations". And now there's a fresh detail. It says your daughter twice sought refuge this past year in a maidservant's bed, Miss Mercy Boyle, to avoid . . . and again the word used in the report is "molestation".'

Oh Mercy, Mercy, Mercy, tattling my idiocies and privacies to Shanley? Have you betrayed me, girl?

Billy Winters' voice was scarcely audible as he asked:

'Have you tortured me enough, Sir?'

Fairbrother paused on his way to the door:

'You know where to come if you find out anything. Ask for Chief Inspector Mallon.'

'You can find your way to hell, Fairbrother, if they'll have you.'

Maurice Fairbrother shrugged slightly, opened the office door and let himself out into the early-evening light. There was a crack followed by an earth rumble as five thousand tonnes of limestone collapsed along fifty yards of quarry face causing a vibration at the office window, and sudden twilight as dust shut out the view of lake, field and sky.

8

For half an hour now the afternoon sun had dipped behind the black mass of cloud, making the requiem of daffodils seem unnaturally livid under greening beech. High above the apple blossom, the air was tense with the screech and swoop of swallows. Are they early or late? Arriving the day I leave. Where from? Spain? Africa? My favourite sound long ago and now. Is it mating or eating, or the joy of coming back? Same families coming since the house was built. Two hundred summers of swallows. More? Thousands of them on the outhouses, on the stone ridge-tiles of the yard, on barns, garden walls, guttering. Every September the place alive with them before leaving . . . waving to them as a child from Mother's bedroom . . . Goodbye swallows, lucky swallows, goodbye, goodbye . . . see you next summer. After tomorrow there's no returning . . . ever; goodbye, goodbye.

There was an alarm clock on a bedside table alongside a vase of bluebells, and a book of William Carleton's, *Traits and Humours of the Irish Peasantry*. The story 'Wild Goose Lodge' she had read last night, a story based on fact and so disturbing she lay awake for hours trying to exorcise it from her mind.

She could hear Mercy clattering below at the stove, wetting and sugaring a gallon of golden-brown tea, buttering and jamming wedges of soda bread, peeling the brown hard-boiled eggs for men in the bog. She'll be up soon to call me. Do I tell her I'm going? Of course. When? How? On our way to the bog? On the way back? Tonight? *She* might lie awake then and make everything awkward. Send her home for a few days? Yes . . . that's it. She'd jump at that. Not sure what I'll say till I say it. When she comes in now she'll see and know I haven't been resting. She'll wonder what I've been doing for two hours.

She prised off her shoes and lay on the bed coverlet, her heart a stumbling counterpoint to the tick of the alarm as she tried not to think of the coming night, the dawn to follow, the train and boat journey. Once again during the last two hours she had counted her money: twenty-two pounds and twelve shillings, enough to take her to America and back twice; two cases, one full of gold. The gold was never far from her mind. When talking with Ward the words used were 'take' or 'get'; when I 'take', when we 'get' the gold. In fact, she knew the word was 'steal'. When I steal, when I rob, with stealth, with cunning, I then become a thief, a robber, a guilty person, deserving of condemnation in a Court of Law, deserving only jail, humiliation, punishment. Do I understand what I am risking tonight? Am I in my right mind, or just stupid?

Why risk everything with one move? A punishment for Billy Winters for the beatings and humiliations overheard long ago, for using me as a dairymaid-cum-housekeeper, for the drunken gropings, for the shameful suggestions. Do I hate him enough to take such a risk. Do I hate him at all? Sometimes. And do I love Liam

Ward? I'm besotted. Yes, but do I love? Now that the hour of stealing was close, it was a lot more frightening than when planned three weeks before.

She could be arrested on arrival in Belfast, or boarding the Glasgow or Liverpool boat. The more she thought about this, the more she realised that possession of the gold would mean a kind of continuous terror about the degradation of being caught and imprisoned. 'Take it,' Ward had said, 'we'll bury it and you stay on, brazen it out.' Not possible. The Constabulary asking questions. Billy's eyes boring into her growing unease. He might not suspect at first, but in time her guilt would grow with his suspicion. In any case, she couldn't act. On stage once at school she had almost fainted when she had to utter two lines, as a messenger in *The Merchant of Venice*.

There was a knock at the door. Mercy Boyle came into the room and placed a cup of steaming tea on the bedside table. Beth swung her legs to the floor and remained sitting on the side of the bed.

'You didn't pull the curtains, Miss?'

'It was too beautiful outside.'

Clear-eyed, Mercy looked into Beth's glazed eyes:

'Did you sleep itself?'

'I dozed a little, I think.'

'You still look wore out.'

'I'm all right.'

As Mercy moved to the window and looked out, a small gust loosened thousands of beech husks into a brown flurry soundlessly tumbling against slates, windows and walls and on downwards into the maze of wistaria running the length of the house:

'Oh God! Look Miss, could anything be nicer?'

Beth looked out.

'It's like heaven,' Mercy added.

Both women stared at the fawn snow against beech green and the navy of sky till Beth asked:

'Where then is hell?'

'The pong of porter and dirty socks in Mickey Dolphin's room. God knows when that cratur last washed himself . . . Men are filthy, dirty devils.'

Mercy turned and stared into Beth's smiling face:

'All's ready below Miss, you don't have to come.'

'I want to.'

Mercy picked up Carleton. Beth could see her spelling the title, pronouncing the words in her head:

'Traits?'

'That's right,' Beth said: *'Traits and Humours of the Irish Peasantry'*.

'Peasantry! I'd be one of those!'

'It means a countryperson.'

'And traits,' Mercy persisted, 'is that like a picnic, an outing?'

'Oh no, no,' Beth said. 'You could say hospitality is our best-known trait, laziness our worst.'

'Aye, or spite, or gettin' mad-drunk.'

'Or superstition.'

'What's the plain word for that, Miss?'

'Pishogues,' Beth said.

'I'm sick of *them*.' Half the girls of the country were looking down wells last week to see the face of the man they'd marry . . . Eejits!'

'Did you do that, Mercy?'

'There was worse torture in our house . . . every May Eve up to this our old one made me and the sisters wash our hands and faces in our own pish, to scare off the fairies; true as God, Miss. In the end we ganged up agin her and said, "to hell with the fairies". Even so, she lies awake in fright on the every May Eve.'

Mercy flicked over some pages of Carleton:

'Is these good yarns?'

'I've only read one: "Wild Goose Lodge".'

'Is it good?'

'Terrible.'

'Teedjus?'

'No, frightening.'

'God, I'd love that; we'll read that together some night.'

Beth glanced at the time on the alarm clock. Seeing her do this Mercy said:

'Aye . . . we should shape to go, Miss.' In the kitchen they divided evenly the carrying of cans, crockery and baskets, crossed the upper yard and went through an entry leading to the lower yard. Beyond an arch on their left, in an outhouse, they could see Albert through the fine wire mesh of a half-door. He was upside-down, a potato in his mouth to allow clearance of the blood dripping into a large earthenware crock on the stone floor. Tomorrow Blinky Blessing would come back to gut and dismember for salting or smoking. Both girls avoided looking at the slaughtered pig. It was Mercy who spoke first:

'You'd wonder sometimes,' she said, 'about killin' craturs at all.'

'Small wonder,' Beth said, 'we seem good at it.'

'Poor Albert. When he saw Blinky and our three men, he started to screech. I kep telling him lies, kep saying "it's all right, Albert, it's all right." Then Blinky did the business.' She paused and muttered:

'A bad dog, that fella.'

'There's no harm in him,' Beth said.

'And less good . . . He asked me for a porringer in the yard . . . I didn't know what he wanted it for so I got it. Then he cut Albert's throat, filled the porringer with blood and drank it down hot. I was fair sick, I can tell you, but I wouldn't plaze him to show it. And all the silly spakes out of him: "that beats Arthur Guinness" and "that's the boy id grow hairs on your Mickey" and all our men laughing and telling him he was "a holy terror and a fright to the world" . . . He's a right sickener. Then when Albert was hung up, and our men gone, he said "How's about a belt of a coort, Mercy." Then he angled me into a corner and began to push agin me. I pushed him off very wicked and told him all he'd get from me was a thick ear. Then he blocked the door, put his hand in his pocket and started in to jiggle and ogle so I said: "Is that what you be at every night above when you're saying the Rosary with Blind Wishie and Mammywee!" Didn't shame him a bit! He just went on jigglin', so I lifted the crock of blood. "If you don't quit that carry-on," I said, "I'll smash this over your head"; I meant it. That shifted him. I'll not tell you the names he called after me . . . A bad dog that fella, and my father says bad dogs should be put down.'

'You'd wonder sometimes,' Beth said, 'about killin' craturs at all.'

It took ten seconds for her irony to register. Then they were both laughing.

To get to the bog-pass from the yards they had to go through the low end of the haggard, through a gap into the rushes of the gut bottom, then down into poorish pasture of thorn and rabbit warren into a wilderness of alder scrub, birch and cut-over bog: the type of landscape comprising the bulk of Ward's thirty acres at Brackagh. The pass now began to slope down through a flame of whins. Faraway they could hear the pulse of a corncrake. Beyond the birch and alder, mirrored in pools about a quarter of a mile away, they could see the black figures of three men, one wheeling a barrow to spread out turf, another catching and loading a second barrow; the third man, Jim Ruttledge most likely, out of sight on the floor of the bog, cutting and throwing sods with one flowing movement, a turf sod in mid-air every five seconds or so.

The bog-pass now dwindled down to a narrow track merging into the bog and established year after year by the traffic of cart-wheels, barrows and slipes. Now on the flat they could no longer see down to the turf bench where the men were working and were forced to go singly to avoid stumbling on tussocks of bluegrass and heather. Every now and then they had to bend to avoid briars, low-growing alder and sally. Yellow catkins powdered their hair and dresses. When they stooped to avoid branches, the smell of bog rosemary filled their heads, its orangey bloom vivid as the creamy florets of emerging meadowsweet. The sun had reappeared. It was hot for early May, and the baskets and cans which had seemed light in the yard now dragged at their arms. The buttermilk was in a heavy metal can and Beth offered to swop. Mercy said no and suggested sitting a minute; Beth agreed. At a small clearing with tree stumps they put down the cans and baskets and sat leaning back against the stumps.

Beth sat looking down on Mercy stretched out and wondered would this perhaps be a good time to broach her leavetaking, and thought: no ... it's too sunny; I'll wait till we're on our way back to the house. She was about to close her eyes against the brightness when she saw something move in the bracken ten yards away. A second later a half-grown fox cub emerged, a raffish cunning snout that almost seemed to be smiling. Two other cubs joined it. They stared a while at the girls, decided there was no danger, and began to frisk and mock-fight: pranking, tumbling and racing in circles. Beth watched fascinated. Very slowly, she moved her hand towards Mercy's shoulder, squeezing it gently. Mercy opened her eyes, stared across the clearing and whispered:

'I declare to God!'

They were both still watching when they felt the ground vibrate followed by a heavy rumbling from the direction of the quarry. The cubs were gone before the rumble became silence. Mercy half-pushed up onto her elbow staring after the cubs:

'Nice wee playboys,' she said, 'give them a month and they'll be villains; it's bred in them.'

She lay back closing her eyes again.

'I suppose,' Beth said, 'we should go.'

'Go, go, go! The mother says it's a class of slavery.'

'What is?' Beth asked.

'All the "go" what we're at now and every day, slaves to the fire, luggin' grub miles to feed men, baking and boiling and cooking, and sloisterin' with buckets and mops, Sunday to Sunday, Christmas to Christmas: men, dogs, pigs, hens, cats, calves and then childer till they're fit to fend for theirselves and then we're fit for nothin' but the chair in the corner or the box in the ground. "It's a wonder to God," she said, "there aren't more hoors in the world: it's a short life they have, but more sport in one week than most of us have in a lifetime!" Then she said, "God forgive me, I could be damned for sayin' the like," so we all prayed the beads twice over that night so as the Mammy wouldn't burn for praisin' hoors!'

Through laughter, Beth said:

'If we hadn't this to lug to the bog, we'd have missed the smell of whins and the May blossom and the sun in the fields, and the fox cubs and talking here like this. She could be right though, your mother, in a way.' Mercy opened her eyes squinting up at Beth:

'Oh you'd need to be fierce brassy for the like of that, and begging your pardon, Miss, but I'd make a better hoor than you.'

As they were both laughing again Beth said:

'I'm going to miss you, Mercy Boyle.'

Mercy swivelled round staring up as Beth added:

'When we *do* part.'

'Part? I'm two townlands off . . . that's no woeful parting, is it? Unless you're for off somewhere far?'

Beth moved and began to pick up a basket and can saying:

'This tea'll be tepid; they don't like it that way.'

'Are you Miss?'

'We'll talk later.'

'Goin' somewhere?'

'We'll talk later.'

When they came to the cutting bank, there was no one in sight. They could see one barrow loaded ready for wheeling and spreading, the other empty. High above, a curlew wheeled fluting, desolate, faraway. Its mate replied closer. On an upside-down slipe, they placed the cans of buttermilk, tea and baskets of bread, cold bacon and eggs. They could hear the men's voices coming up from the floor of the bog. Mercy went to the edge of the bank to call them. The three men were about twelve feet down. Jim Ruttledge seemed to be digging sideways into the face of the bog with his slane. Mickey Dolphin hunkering, watched. Mercy's brother Gerry was on all fours, peering to see what Jim Ruttledge was digging out.

'What are yis at?' Mercy called down.

No one answered. Mickey Dolphin glanced up and motioned with his hand, much as to say, 'not now' or 'go away' or both. Mercy went back to Beth:

'Don't pour yet, Miss, they're scobin' into the bank. They've found somethin' or they're after somethin'.'

'Did they say what?'

Mercy shook her head. Both women now went over and looked down. Mickey Dolphin looked up:

'Jim's hit on something; he has it near out.'

'What is it?' Mercy asked.

'A go of auld bog-butter . . . or maybe someone was murdered long ago; not gold, that's for sure.'

There were five, deep, rough-cut steps shaped out of the bank. The girls went down and stood watching Jim Ruttledge who had now hived a neat bole over what looked like a lump of wet black leather. With both hands, he was taking out fistfuls of blackish debris clinging to the back, top and sides of the buried bulk. He then put both arms around his find, removed it and walked toward the steps. All followed. The wrapping leather was removed revealing butter which looked white as lard, mottled with tiny black and green choppings of herb. Each of the men in turn hooked a forefinger or nail into the butter and smelled, wrinkling their noses. When Beth and Mercy did the same, they looked at each other:

'I'd as lief take dry bread,' Mercy said.

'There's wild garlic in it,' Beth said, smelling again.

'Aye,' Jim Rutledge said, 'the men and weemen that milked the cows, and buried this, are dust this brave time theirselves.'

'They'd be quare and agey if they weren't,' said Mickey Dolphin.

All laughed and Mickey went on, as mugs of tea and food were passed around:

'I seen me above in the home place and we dug up a wad of butter and it twice as big as this one here.'

'*Twice* as big?' Jim Rutledge asked.

'Aye,' Mickey said, 'and sour too like this, and there come two men up from Dublin, scholars they were, to view it and weigh it and they had to see where it was dug, and then they had to trick and test and measure and God knows what all, and in the latter end one scholar, the younger man, declared it could be buried there before Saint Patrick come here. The auld man, the professor, he stepped farther back, "it could be down there," says he, "before Christ came into the world, at all, at all".'

'Maybe those wise men should be told about this find,' Jim Ruttledge said winking.

'For why?' Mickey asked. 'To be tortured with questions? It's no buried child, it's a lump of butter; we don't need codgers in bowler hats to tell us what we know: it's bog-butter.'

'What'll you do with it, Jim?' Mercy asked.

Jim Ruttledge pushed the turf barrow sideways, put a smear of the bog-butter on the axle bearings and spun the wheel:

'That's all it's fit for now: greasing axles and feedin' pigs.'

'Poor Albert missed that feed!' Mickey said. 'And didn't he go off horrid noisy in the end.'

'You'd be noisy too,' Jim Ruttledge said, 'if there was three men holdin' you down for Blinky to cut your throat.'

After laughter and out of nowhere, Gerry Boyle said:

'March'll search'
'And April try'
'It's May'll tell'
'If you live or die.'
'If that's true,' Jim Ruttledge said, 'pray God we stagger on to the month of June.'

Tea was poured. The men sat and wiped sweat from their eyes with sleeves and shirt-tails. Beth added sugar to the mugs, stirring. The early-evening sun was in the bog and a cool wind came from the north; weather to dry turf without the labour of turning. The men's faces were reddened by sun, arms scorched to the elbow, eyes dazed from work. Nobody said anything much till they had eaten all the food in the baskets and drunk three or four mugs of tea each. High above the slurping, eating and burping, the curlew wheeled, piping. Shading their eyes against the sun, the girls looked up. They could not see it against the blinding brightness. Neither began to eat or drink until the men were replete. When they did, the talk was of bog-finds and infanticide, of Parnell and Lord Leitrim, of Percy French and Martin Luther, of pishogues and miracles, of cockfights and hunts, of the power of the priests, of the weather, of horses, of Lord Erne's new American bride at Crom Castle, of America itself, of emigration, of the caves under the ground where they sat and the mad Frenchman down there mapping them, of cures and remedies for the jaundice, the sprain, the shingles, the piles, for sterility, the wonder of wells, mountains and fountains, the tragedy of the old famine of forty-eight, of the present near-famine in the west.

As always, there was edginess between Mickey Dolphin and Jim Ruttledge; some of it good-natured, some of it less so. When it was learned that Mickey would be leaving the bog early to get ready for Enniskillen and the

Percy French concert, Jim Ruttledge's spikiness became obvious.

Mickey was saying that old Grue the hedgemaster told him once it was an Irishman showed the Roman engineers how to make the great roads of the empire.

'How is it,' said Jim Ruttledge, 'we've such poor sign of them here?'

'If we had the reins in our own hands,' Mickey said, 'you'd see silver chariots here on golden roads to blind the world.'

'More like,' says Jim Ruttledge, 'you'd make a hames of the whole show . . . that's if you were fit to *make* a hames.'

There was laughter which Mickey did not join. After quite a silence he said:

'Now there's a thing.'

'What *thing* is that?' Jim Ruttledge asked drily.

'There's a man and that man's not too far from here; you could say straight out he was in this bog. You can go stronger and say he's close-by; he's here.'

'Giveover the wandery talk, Mickey; spake your spake, say out what's in your head.'

Mickey Dolphin was not to be deflected from the shape, pace and intention of what was in his head, and how he wanted to tell it:

'One night that man above in the kitchen at Clonoula said: "Your Pope in Rome could be a construction, he could be a made-up thing, a make-believe, a class of scarecrow."'

'That sounds like me,' Jim Ruttledge said smiling.

Mickey turned to Beth:

'You were three years down there, below Rome, Miss, you can tell us now: is the Pope a scarecrow or God's first and proper man?'

'The Pope,' Beth said, 'is the Bishop of Rome.'

'Did ever you see him?' Mickey asked.

'Once, with a hundred thousand other people.'

'And could you see his face, could you look in his eyes?'

'He was very far away, like a small white cloud.'

Jim Ruttledge was pursing his lips to suppress open grinning:

'It's the roundy-hatted lads,' he said, 'in the purple frocks, *they* poke the fire; the Pope's only a puff of smoke.'

'And what could an auld black Protestant like you know about the lek of that?'

For a moment the talk seemed to cross the ditch of banter into the sheugh of insult. Jim Ruttledge refused to respond. He took his time before saying:

'I know enough to stay away . . . to stand on my own hind legs and think for myself. I'm not on my knees; I'm free to say: "that's alright . . . or . . . that's a cod".'

'Are you saying our Pope's a cod?'

'More of a whale,' Jim Ruttledge muttered.

In the laughter that followed, Mickey Dolphin was too annoyed to enjoy the teasing. Determined not to lose the argument he turned again to Beth for help:

'What do you say Miss?'

She looked from Jim Ruttledge's weathered face that seemed cut out of wood or stone, to Mickey Dolphin's doggy bloodshot eyes under a fringe of black hair:

'Does any of it matter?' she asked.

Jim Ruttledge said very quickly:

'Oh be God it matters, it matters who's in charge and it matters to the death.'

Gerry Boyle smiled now, showing his brilliant white teeth as he stuttered out:

'Meadowsweet to bring on sleep
And burdocks for the ass.'

His mouth stayed open foolishly as he stared at his sister. Clearly he had forgotten the lines that followed. Mercy prompted without looking at him: 'No thatch can rot . . .'

'No thatch can rot,' Gerry continued, 'on keep or cot that heeds the holy Mass.'

'There's your answer,' Mickey Dolphin said.

Jim Ruttledge lit his pipe very deliberately before saying:

'If there was an ass in charge of the world, it might run a bit sweeter!'

During this talk Beth and Mercy had tipped the dregs out of mugs and packed them in a basket, gathered up crusts, replaced lids on cans of tea and buttermilk. Mickey Dolphin asked for the time. Jim Ruttledge took out his pocket-watch and said it was just gone half-past five . . . then both Mickey and Mercy began to rib him. Would he talk with plain people after 'the grandeur' of this outing? Would he be wearing his navy-blue Sunday suit or his black funeral overcoat? Would he have time to milk the cows before leaving? And certainly he could carry a share of the tea-things back to the kitchen and not leave empty handed. Jim Ruttledge leaned over and whispered in his ear:

'If you're in charge of the gig, Mickey, take care; it's not the blind drunk driving the blind drunk!'

'I can handle myself,' Mickey said aloud.

'I don't doubt that,' said Jim Ruttledge.

All watched him leave, loaded with empty cans and baskets, heading up out of the bog, a small neat man trying to walk with dignity, aware that he was being watched by smiling observers and because of this his walk was somehow comical. Jim Ruttledge stood suddenly, saying:

'We've three hours of light left; that's two weeks' winter burning . . . come on son,' he said to Gerry Boyle.

'You've done well, Jim,' Beth said.

'One lucky day can make all the difference,' said Jim Ruttledge.

Now, in the evening, on the way back, the sight and smell of May blossom was so pervasive that they stopped from time to time to take it in.

'I could look at this forever,' Mercy said.

Now, Beth thought, I'll have to tell her now. Mercy had stopped. Beth had walked on a few steps. She turned and said:

'I'm leaving, Mercy, early tomorrow, and I'll not be back . . . and I doubt if I'll see you again. I couldn't leave without telling you this, without saying goodbye.'

Mercy's mouth was open. Her eyes began to glaze over as she swallowed before saying:

'That's put very bare; you'll have to give me a track more, Miss.'

'I can't.'

'Does the boss know?'

Beth shook her head. They walked in silence for a minute.

'He'll grieve something awful . . . When you're gone for a day it's "Miss Beth this and Miss Beth that" . . . "Have you told Miss Beth" . . . "we don't want to worry Miss Beth" . . . betimes it can be a quare sickener; the man dotes on you.'

'That's partly why I'm leaving.'

'It'll break the man's heart,' Mercy said, then added, 'and mine.'

Almost overcome, she turned away:

'You're havin' me on, Miss?'

Beth shook her head.

'There's no head nor tail, no sense to it.'

'There is.'

'Are you not happy here?'

'I'd be happier elsewhere.'

'You think.'

'Yes, I do.'

After another silence, Mercy blurted:

'You're never runnin' off with a fella?'

The question was so unexpected, it caused a startled blush which Beth's 'don't be silly' could not hide. There was no avoiding Mercy's astonished eyes staring now with disbelief:

'Jesus,' she uttered, 'you are! . . . you're elopin' . . . You're gone all red, Miss! You're runnin' off with a fella . . . are you?'

Mercy continued to stare:

'It's never any of them dull dogs the boss brings out betimes?'

Beth shook her head.

'Is it anybody . . . I know?'

Beth looked straight back into Mercy's eyes and lied:

'It's no one anyone knows . . . least of all me.'

Mercy now knew she would not be told:

'This is the quare turnabout . . . If you leave here I won't stay one day, that's for certain . . . nor one night, that's more certain.'

Far away they could hear Billy Winters shouting. Both their names: 'Beth! Mercy!'

'Whisht,' Mercy said, 'there's the boss.'

'I heard,' Beth said. 'There's a salad set out for him.'

'Someone'll have to wet him a pot of tea.'

'He'll not bother with tea this evening' Beth said, and added, 'let him drink whiskey.'

Mercy bit her lip and giggled. In three years working at Clonoula she had never once heard Beth being disrespectful.

Again the voice called out:

'Beth! . . . Mercy!'

'I should go, Miss . . . maybe he wants his shoes polished.'

'If you want . . . I'll bring in the cows.'

They parted at a point in the beechwood where the ground was level with the roof of Clonoula. They could see rooks and daws circling high above the chimney stacks, alert and startled by the sudden sharpness of the human voice calling in the yard far below.

9

Mickey Dolphin stood in the yard looking down sideways at the cobbles, a bird listening for worms. Billy Winters stared through the yard entry in the direction of the bog and shouted yet again:

'Mercy! . . . Beth!'

'Where in hell are they, Mickey? If they left the bog just after you why in hell aren't they here now?'

'Could be they stopped on to help spread.'

'You get washed and togged, eat something and we'll go.'

Billy crossed the yard, went in the back door, into the scullery and through to the kitchen. Its bareness and cleanliness angered him. One place at the scrubbed deal table was set for Mickey Dolphin. He tipped up a covering plate and looked: two boiled eggs split, radishes, chives and a slice of cold boiled bacon. From where he stood he could see through the hallway to the dining-room where a place was set for him at the top of the table identical to the place set for Mickey Dolphin. Once in the early years during an upset she had left saying 'I prefer to eat with my own people,' and he had muttered, 'Aye . . . and lie with them.'

She had stood very still, her hand on the door handle for what seemed like a minute before saying, 'That's low,' and he had answered, 'You've said it woman; and true.'

Two decades later her clenched face still came back vividly. Why now did the two meal places set so neatly fill him with a kind of anger. Miss Beth; miscegenation; misbegotten! He lifted the silver cover, took a portion of cold bacon, stuffed it into his mouth and moved, chewing, to unlock the sideboard cupboard. He then brought a bottle of Locke's Irish Whiskey and a tumbler to the table. He half-filled the tumbler and, still chewing, went out to the scullery for water.

Mickey Dolphin, a faded towel round his waist, was filling a tin ewer from a very slow copper tap. He stepped aside to allow Billy to fill the small glass jug with water.

'Hurry on man, fill her up.'

Mickey put the ewer under the tap again. It seemed to fill very slowly:

'Poor pressure,' Mickey said, 'on account of the dry time, the fountain must be low.'

As both stared at the flowing water, Billy became conscious of a marked personal odour, a summer dormitory smell. He glanced down at Mickey's feet: they were a dirty grey colour.

'Did you ever hear, Mickey, about the auld fella who went to the doctor . . . a bit of a hum off him, so the doctor told him to wash. He did that and came back; still there was a hum.'

'"Did you wash at all?"' the doctor asked him.

'"I did," the auld fella said.

'"How," asked the doctor.

'"Up as far as possible," says he, "and down as far as possible."'

'"Go back so," said the doctor, and wasn possible:

Both laughed, Billy a great deal louder and longer. As he crossed the yard to the loft bedroom over the coach house he called after Mickey:

'Be sure and wash possible, Mickey.'

On the way back to the dining-room the smile went from Billy Winters' face as he topped the tumbler with water and stood looking out the window, as he had looked out every day since childhood. Trying not to think, he closed his eyes, moved away from the window and began glancing from object to object. On an upright Blüthner piano there was a goldfish bowl full of coral shells from a beach in Connemara alongside a vase of narcissi mixed with sprigs of beech in leaf. Between these, a silver-framed photograph of Cathy taken two months before her death, a face that now seemed haunted, as though she had an instinct or premonition of the terrible end awaiting her. He could never look at it without emotion, and avoided looking now. On the wall above the piano there was a sampler hand-stitched by his mother with flowers at the top and a sundial at the bottom. He knew it heart and now spoke it aloud biting out each word:

'A garden is a lovesome thing
God wot
Rose plot
Fringed pool
Ferned grot
The veriest school
Of peace; and yet the fool
Maintains that God is not.
Not God in gardens
When the eve

is cool?
Nay but I have a sign.
'Tis very sure he walks in mine'

Billy Winter quaffed a large mouthful of whiskey and muttered:

'Aye, and the devil too!'

Beside the portrait of his grandfather, stony-eyed and holding the beaver cap in his hands, there was a calendar with a pencil mark through all the dead days including today, Thursday May 3rd 1883 . . . Mr Percy French, renowned . . . in the Town Hall Enniskillen . . . Mr Keats, famous English poet . . . deceased . . . death and nightingales. Contrary as her mother and as devious, how could she be otherwise, begat in the viper's bowels, in sheugh, hovel or loft; a poisonous replica. Behold her single in the field? Behold her coupled in the ditch with a proven thief? A suspected murderer?

He was pouring again, topping the whiskey up with water, a flush of temper spreading over his face and neck as he jerked a glance at the portrait of William Hudson Winters and asked matter-of-factly:

'What do you think, William? Am I an empty shell in a goldfish bowl to be spied on by a maidservant, reported to Constabulary, questioned by an Englishman? So much for Christmas bribes to the barracks, stout for the Constables, whiskey for the Sergeant. What does it add to? A bucket of piss! And who informed? Mercy's knight in blue, her Constable companion, shit Shanley, Seamus Grin Shanley, her well informed, uniformed informer?'

Suddenly he shouted very loudly, his voice carrying through the dining-room window:

'Where in hell are they!'

Mickey Dolphin's voice came back from the loft window across the yard:

'I see Mercy, Sorr, from here, Sorr, she's comin' down through the wood beside the haggard . . . she'll be five minutes off at most.'

'And Miss Beth?'

'Mercy's alone, Sorr.'

'Alone, is she? . . . and pray where is your gentle mistress Mercy? Do you know? Do I know? Does God know? The devil does for sure: with a conniving rat, a mongrel-eyed, thieving, skulking son of Cain; my Fenian gale-hung tenant of Brackagh, Liam Ward.'

A sudden involuntary trembling brought tears to his eyes:

'Ass haltered all my days to a brace of devious scheming clats! If the goldfish can be gawked at in the bowl . . . he can gawk back at the gawkers!'

He then shouted loudly:

'Mickey!'

'Yes, Sorr.'

'Can you still see her?'

'I can, Sorr.'

'Where is she now?'

'Crossin' the yard.'

'Are you ready?'

'I've shaved and washed . . . I've done . . . all possible.'

'Get Punch in the gig, bring him up to the front and wait.'

'Yes, Sorr.'

At the back door Mickey Dolphin met Mercy Boyle and whispered:

'Christ, Mercy, he's like a bag of weasels inside, shoutin' after you a fright.'

'We heard . . . for why, Mickey?'

Mickey shook his head and shrugged:

'Whatever it is he's in there talkin' to himself, worse again he's tellin' jokes . . . a sure sign he's in wicked form.'

As Mercy took off her field boots in the scullery, she heard Billy Winters' voice: edgy:

'That you, Mercy?'

'Yes, Sorr.'

'Can I see you a minute?'

'I'm comin', Sorr.'

There was a strong hum of whiskey in the room. She could see the bottle, the jug of whiskey, the empty glass on the dining-room table. For what seemed like a minute or longer he kept her standing on the pitchpine surround near the door. Not knowing what to do with her hands she found herself feeling the buttons of her smock, aware that he was angry, that she was about to be questioned, reprimanded or both. To quell the beating of her heart, she kept telling herself, Its no matter . . . I don't give a tinker's snot what he says; it's the last time I'll have to stand like this and be dressed down . . . no woman body in this house tomorrow to drudge in kitchen or dairy, to wash his shirts, empty his pots and boil his spuds . . .

Although she was afraid she felt a little sorry for him, and he could see from the set of his face that whatever was in his head was making him very angry. When he did speak he looked at his feet and his voice was unexpectedly soft:

'You brought tea to the bog, Mercy?'

'We did, Sorr, yes.'

'How did they manage today?'

'There's a sight of stuff spread, Sorr, tomorrow'll see the end of it; they wrought well.'

'That's good.'

'The weather's been lucky.'

'Yes.'

There was another protracted pause. This time Billy Winters looked straight into Mercy's eyes and kept looking:

'Have you anything to tell me, Mercy?' Mercy searched about in her head:

'Jim Ruttledge found a go of bog-butter.'

'Did he?'

'Twelve feet down or more, he's goin' to get Blessing's ass to bring it up here tonight . . . it smells rotten.'

'A secret burial?'

'Yes, Sorr.'

'And smells rotten.'

'Yes, Sorr.'

'Most buried secrets are dug up in the end, you know that?'

'I do, Sorr.'

'Nothin's hidden forever in this world.'

Billy Winters looked away and then said:

'This way or that way, the truth will out . . . isn't that so, Mercy?'

'Yes, Sorr.'

'And where is Miss Beth now?'

'Gone for the cows I'd say.'

'Have you anything else to tell me, Mercy?'

'Well . . . Blinky Blessing come after dinner and Albert got the business . . . He's below in the old dairy with a spud in his mouth.'

'A Blessing in disguise?'

'Yes, Sorr.'

'For Albert . . . Death comes to us all this way or that, isn't that so, Mercy?'

'Yes, Sorr.'

'You fell on your knees to kiss Mr Parnell's hand when he walked into this house two months ago, remember?'

'Yes, Sorr.'

'Has he housed you, fed you, paid you, forgone rent for years on end, helped your family in every possible way, employed your disadvantaged brother?'

'No, Sorr.'

'No. Have *I* been unkind to you ever?'

'No, Sorr.'

'Well then? Who would you pick between, the Fenian betrayer James Carey or the Christ-betrayer, Judas Iscariot?'

Mercy could see from the veins pulsing down his neck that he was barely composed and was now moving out of control as he bit out each word.

'I don't know what you want me to say, Sorr.'

'Not *say* . . . Mercy; *tell* . . . you *tell* me now what you've told about me outside this house; the malice, the slander, the lies.'

He shouted the word 'lies' so loudly that she felt her hand moving to her mouth:

'Why are you hiding your mouth, girl? We all blunder from time to time but some blunders are beyond forgiveness.'

'I done nothin', Sorr, said nothin' 'bout you to anyone.'

'And now you lie to my face . . . Time was you'd be whipped for that girl, and will be when I get back . . . if you're not gone, you and your gulpin' brother.'

The word 'gulpin'' smarted as sharply as a slap on the face, bringing tears to her eyes. She was tempted to say 'You'd be a sorry man if you did the like, 'cause my father can pull a cow from a sheugh on his own and I have four strong brothers who are not 'gulpins''.

Before she could answer, Billy Winters was gone through the dining-room door that led to the hall and front door to where Mickey Dolphin was waiting with the gig ready to draw away. She was conscious that the room had become blurred and that her whole body was trembling with fear and outrage.

Mickey Dolphin had heard the shouting from the dining-room and the word 'lies'. He avoided looking at Billy Winters as he stepped into the gig, causing it to tip sideways and creak on its springs. Talk would have to wait until they were well down the avenue. Far beyond Dacklin and Brackagh and the Cuilcagh Mountains, the western sun was drowning in the blood of the Lower Lough. Mickey now saw Billy Winters take two tickets from the inside pocket of his jacket. He looked at them without seeing them, flicked them angrily with a forefinger and replaced them in his pocket. He then stared at the sinking sun.

As the gig approached the gatelodge, Beth emerged from behind a cattle drinking-well framed by whitethorn and elderbush. She paused to look down as twelve cows continued to plod across the side of the hill in the direction of the house and yard. She shaded her eyes to look down, looking and not wanting to look lest she would have to wave with both arms as she had done dozens of times as a child.

Billy Winters kept staring ahead towards the gatelodge lest she would see him looking up and begin to wave. Never, ever again. She had thrown herself away, shamefully, deliberately, secretly. There would be no more waving, no false farewells. He would say nothing. He would watch and wait, listen to her lies, glide and hover above and when the time was right, swoop and tear her treachery to pieces.

It seemed monstrous to him now that she was standing exactly where his mother had stood, about this time of year thirty years ago. She had been gathering elder blossom, had taken off her straw hat and waved down. He and his father had waved back and the seemingly foolish calling had echoed and re-echoed up and down and across the fields, bye, bye, bye, bye, bye . . . God be with you. Jim Ruttledge had found her unconscious an hour later and carried her to the house: She had recovered enough to talk a little, and say: 'Then throw me away!'

As they passed the gatelodge, Winnie Ruttledge waved from a clothesline. Billy Winters and Mickey Dolphin returned the greeting as the gig went through the globe-topped piers and turned right down the street past a row of single-storeyed thatched dwellings, one of them two-storeyed, the post office-cum-public house and grocery. Barefoot children playing on the street were careful not to let Billy Winters see their protruding tongues, the single- and double-thumb nose salutes, the carefully subdued tongue-farts. Billy could read these antics in Mickey Dolphin's eyes and pursed lips:

'What are they at, Mickey?'

'You know yourself, childer, shapes and faces.'

'What about?'

'It's the old quarrel, Billy Sorr . . . Mr Parnell has the whole country set agin' every breed of landlord.'

Last Sunday, the London *Times* had been gloomy about Ireland. Evictions, rack-renting, hunger, murder, and class hatred seemed likely to continue for the fore-seeable future. An anonymous source quoted Parnell as saying: '"The murder of Lord Frederick in the Phoenix Park and its aftermath, the hanging one by one of the

Fenian 'invincibles', had set back the clock in Ireland for a hundred years or more. A people who could produce such murderers as the 'invincibles' were about as fit to rule themselves as hottentots." Is this the same man who said frequently in America, "We in Ireland will not be satisfied until we have destroyed the last link which keeps us bound to England"? This kind of insane sabre-rattling may please Irish Americans; it also helped to create the murderous "invincibles". Mr Parnell, like it or not, has connived at the murder of Lord Frederick Cavendish.'

'I'm afraid,' Billy said, 'our Mr Parnell is a trouble-maker. God knows where he'll lead us.'

Mickey Dolphin switched the whip across Punch's back and said:

'A while back, Billy Sorr, you told us all he was the greatest man ever you met – maybe the greatest man in the world, at the minute.'

'Great men,' Billy said, 'can be great trouble-makers.'

'Aye! and some little men too, it's the old wrong was never put right.'

'Right or wrong, where were *ye* before *we* came?'

'Where we are now, Billy Sorr, in our own country.'

'And who did *you* put out? And who did *they* put out?'

'A scholar could tell you that, Sorr.'

The road now dipped away from the hamlet of Clonoula down toward the lower lake, now framed in a countryside laced in a glory of whitethorn. Behind them the smoke from the house and cottage chimneys was rising straight up. The weather was due to continue fine from Malin Head to Dingle Bay. *Old Moore's Almanac* was forecasting a dry summer.

Outside the village, two white goats, their front legs roped to one another, caused Mickey Dolphin to tighten on the reins and wait till the goats struggled off sideways towards the ditch:

'Cangled goats,' Billy muttered. 'Are they Blessing's blessed goats?'

'They could be no one else's,' Mickey said.

'In the name of the Father and the Son and the Holy goats,' Billy said dispensing a priestly benediction towards them.

Mickey Dolphin laughed showing gapped brown teeth:

'If you were one of us, Billy Sorr, you'd earn hell for that class of mockery.'

'Can't Protestants earn hell too?'

'They're all goin' there anyway.'

Billy Winters laughed and mock-punched Mickey Dolphin:

'You're in better form this evening Mickey.'

'I am, Sorr.'

'What in God's name was all that this morning?'

'All what, Billy Sorr?'

'All the kneeling and weeping at the bog-hole.'

'That, Sorr?'

'Yes *that* . . . what was in your head?'

'I don't rightly know, Sorr.'

'Can't you tell me?'

'Some day, maybe.'

'Why not now?'

For quite a while Mickey Dolphin did not respond. Billy Winters kept staring, waiting for an answer, forcing Mickey to say: 'On Miss Beth's birthday, May 3rd, a terrible thing happened me . . . a long time ago.'

'Can I hear?'

'I'd rather not, Sorr.'

'That's all right.'

The gig went spanking along the county road, keeping to the line of the loughshore, with a gentle creak of harness, the rhythmic clip of steel on stone. Somewhere an ass trumpeted. They went on through greening fields and meadows under tall roadside trees, through the townlands of Tully, Clonshanco and Dernagola until they reached a straggle of houses outside Enniskillen. On then past the grandiose portals of the Portora Royal School, across the bridge and into the island town. The main street and public houses were thronged with people and horse traffic and everywhere there were posters advertising the visit of Percy French to the Town Hall.

As Mickey Dolphin unharnessed and stabled Punch in the yard of the Imperial Hotel, Billy Winters went into the tavern and ordered a pint of draught Guinness and a scoop of Locke's. They had half an hour. The performance was due to start at seven.

IO

On the second floor of Enniskillen Town Hall Mr Gary Pringle could see, through a gap in the high door, the low platform where Miss Sarah Egerton, organist at St Anne's Church of Ireland, had been playing melodies now for almost half an hour, all of them associated with Mr Percy French. Having exhausted these she was now moving uncertainly to other popular pieces. She sat at an upright piano placed sideways to the audience. To the right of this piano there was a podium ready for Mr French, on which were placed a paraffin lamp, a glass and a decanter full of water. The large reception chamber was full. It was warm, and an usher was trying to open the high, broad windows with a long pole.

The committee members in the lobby downstairs were becoming anxious. Two of them had been to the railway station. Mr French was expected on the six-thirty which he should have caught at Clones junction. He was not on that. They surmised he must be arriving by gig. This information was relayed to Mr Pringle upstairs, who could now see the Protestant Bishop of Clogher looking at his pocket-watch. Aware that Miss Egerton was moving to the concluding chords of 'Carrickfergus', he cleaned his spectacles, adjusted his bow-tie and walked through the high door onto the low platform. Acting-cashier with the Bank of Ireland on the main street, a producer and performer in amateur musicals, he was widely regarded in town and county as something of a wag and raconteur. Standing beside the podium he begged for silence with open hands:

'What we hear about Mr Percy French is that he can be somewhat late but never disappoints. At the moment he is somewhat late. Can we in the meantime not entertain ourselves? I see both Bishops of Clogher here. One is a renowned traveller, a builder of cathedrals and to my certain knowledge has a fine singing voice.'

There was much looking around, until William Armstrong the Protestant Bishop of Clogher, said in clear tones from the second row:

'*That* is most certainly *not me*.'

He had a cold, white face, almond eyes, and kept his mouth fixed in a kind of smile. Attention now moved from the second row to somewhere near the back where James Donnelly, the Catholic Bishop of Clogher, was heard to mutter:

'My God, what a gaffe!' He was seated between his sister and his Curate, Benny Cassidy, who now whispered:

'You'll have to sing now or be damned; you've no choice, he'll torture you till you do.'

Jimmy Donnelly stood and began walking towards the platform amidst tepid clapping from one half of the audience, warm applause from the other. The Earl of Enniskillen, blind grandmaster of the Orange Lodge, inclined his head towards his daughter and asked:

'Can you describe him, dear?'

'He's tiny, Papa, smaller than me and pert with a

pursed-up mouth, white hair and sort of a mincy walk. He's got very good eyes and his suit looks a lot smarter than yours.'

Through the hum of audience expectation Jimmy Donnelly was now consulting with Miss Egerton who had often seen priests in the streets of Enniskillen. Never in her life had she spoken to one. Here now, she was with a Catholic Bishop; her head averted, nodding, her lips moving, Yes she could manage that, yes she knew the song well, yes and that melody too. As her fingers automatically began to phrase a few bars, Jimmy Donnelly turned to the audience and said in a clear tenor voice which was unexpectedly rich and almost accentless:

'The reason I sing occasionally in my garden is because of necessity, when I sing in the house my dog Solomon howls and howls and howls. I think my dog has good judgement.' There was a share of scattered clapping, tolerant smiling and Miss Egerton was obliged to restart the introduction to 'Kathleen Mavoorneen', one of the Bishop's two party pieces, the other being 'Charlie is my darling'. Some said this was a cheeky tilt at his retired predecessor, Charles MacNally, who once said to him coldly at a clerical dinner:

'You're not just silly, Jimmy, you're childish betimes.'

Eight words which still hurt. Those more politically inclined thought it had more to do with his warm approval of the politics of Mr Charles Stewart Parnell.

From the back of the hall an usher now beckoned to Gary Pringle. He went over, listened, nodding and smiling. As he left by the side door Jimmy Donnelly was beginning the first verse of 'Kathleen Mavoorneen'.

It took five minutes to establish that Mr Percy French was coming up the street. By then Jimmy Donnelly was rising emotionally to the last line, his neck craned up as markedly as Miss Egerton's was bent sideways and down towards the soft pedal and the concluding chords. The audience response was genuine and warm.

Gary Pringle smiled, waiting for this to stop. Inclining his head towards Donnelly, he said: 'From what I've just heard, your dog Solomon is a poor judge!'

He waited until the Bishop had retaken his seat and then said:

'I have just received the most agreeable confirmation. Mr Percy French is now in the town and is, as I speak, making his way here with all possible dispatch. He is not, may I hasten to add, as some have suggested, "travelling with Miss Brady in her private ass and cart".'

There was some good-natured laughing.

Outside on the Diamond it was mild for early May, with happily no hint of late-spring sharpness. On account of this, a great many town and country people who could not afford tickets for the performance were waiting to see and welcome Mr French.

Billy Winters and Mickey Dolphin had just come from stabling Punch at the Royal Hotel. As they arrived to the top of the stairs leading to the Town Hall there was a mix of clapping and laughter from lower down the main street. An usher shouted from the lobby:

'He's here! He'll be up directly!' And indeed, there he was, cheerfully doffing his boater to someone waving from a window, shaking hands genially, talking and laughing with people as he moved through the crowd towards the lobby; meeting yet again what he met everywhere: the barefoot world of street and field he wrote and sang about to entertain the booted world that crowded in to hear him in halls and theatres.

After about a minute's delay he emerged from the crowd, mounting the stone steps of the Town Hall, his straw boater in one hand and the other extended towards Billy Winters. Both spoke simultaneously:

'Mv dear fellow.'

'My dear Billy.'

The embrace and handclasps were warm and mutual, but because of the press of people and officials they could not hear each other properly. Billy Winters' invitation to Clonoula could not be accepted:

'No, no, I wish I could . . .'

He glanced back at his wife. She shook her head saying:

'We're booked into Irvinestown . . . We leave straight after.'

Just then Billy Winters realised that Mickey Dolphin was calling him urgently.

'Mr Billy Sorr! Mr Billy Sorr!'

Turning he saw an usher in a bow-tie gripping Mickey's arm above the elbow, escorting him towards the door.

'What in the hell are you at?' Billy called out.

'This hoeboy has no ticket,' the usher said over his shoulder, 'and he's drunk I'd swear.'

'I'd swear he's not, and he's no "hoeboy", he's my friend Michael Dolphin, and this,' Billy said, holding up a small docket, 'is his ticket.'

Percy French adjusted his own bow-tie, leaned towards Billy and said in a whisper:

'One thing for sure I surely know,
Trust no man in a dickie-bow.'

Aloud he said:

'If Michael Dolphin is a friend of my friend Billy Winters then he's a friend of mine.'

With his arm around Mickey Dolphin's shoulder they moved as three from the lobby to the broad staircase leading to the upper hall and straight into the chamber and a tumult of exploding applause. The impression created was of a flamboyant circus performer with his arm around an Indian snake-charmer, with Billy Winters two paces behind . . . a smiling promoter.

Half-way down the aisle, Percy French found a seat for Mickey Dolphin, then paused as a young girl proffered a songbook for his signature. He stooped, bargaining for a kiss which was given before signing. All the while Miss Egerton was playing 'The Darlin' Girl from Clare', addressing the chords with great feeling and flourish, and a side-to-side shaking of her head.

On the platform, Mr Gary Pringle stood beside the podium waiting to introduce Percy French, who now joined him. The response was so sustained that the singer became emotional, and tried once or twice with a wave of the left hand to make it stop. When it did, Gary Pringle moved forward and said:

'It would be impertinent to introduce our guest. Only last week the London *Times* described him as a "phenomenon", an Irishman of Planter stock equally loved by all breeds and creeds of his fellow Irishmen. Ladies and gentlemen, we are all here this evening to welcome to the town of Enniskillen, that phenomenon in person, Mr Percy French, from Frenchpark in the county of Roscommon.

During the applause the singer poured a glass of water from the decanter into the tumbler, drank a mouthful, and Welsh-combed his moustache and hair. When silence came he said, 'I want to begin with a poem for a friend I haven't seen for years. He will know why.'

He then spoke the words of 'Gort-na-Mona' in such a natural unforced voice that people thought at first that he was making a few introductory remarks. When the poem ended he said quickly, 'A sad start, you see, allows me to have a happy ending and I believe in happy endings.' He winked at the audience and began telling them about the West Clare Railway and the origin of the ballad 'Are you right there Michael, are you right', an account they found as hilarious as his eventual singing of the ballad itself.

He then sang 'Phil the Fluther', clowning round the small stage, playing peek-a-boo with Miss Egerton using his banjo as a gun or club, pointing and winking at dignitaries and the audience who now clapped rhythmically as Miss Egerton worked overtime with fingers and pedals and the heels of her sensible shoes. When this piece was concluded, and during the response to it, he took out a handkerchief and wiped his face. He drank more water, waiting for silence:

'Walking up your main street,' he said, 'I saw legends in a few shop windows: "Go to Canada for three pounds by Dominion Line" – and other advertisements for other companies promoting America, Australia, South Africa; shipping lines all competing to take us away from what should be paradise, and I thought: why do we always long to be elsewhere? Do we not belong here? What are we looking for? Glory or a grave? God? Cheap gin? A *new* world? For whatever reason we still leave in our thousands and thousands and this seems to me such heartbreak that I was forced to write a funny song about it.'

Miss Egerton was introducing 'The Mountains of Mourne' again when a young bearded man stood up in the middle of the hall. He had a folded newspaper in one hand and waved it baton-like towards the stage.

Percy French motioned with one hand towards the piano. Miss Egerton stopped playing. Billy Winters, two rows from the front, looked back at the interrupter. He had a monkish face and slight figure, probably one of Parnell's Lieutenants or Davitt's cronies: an agitator, a Land Leaguer, a Fenian crackpot. He could see Mr Gary Pringle urgently beckoning ushers from the back. When the murmur of the audience stopped Percy French said quietly:

'*Yes*, Sir?'

The young man said in a clear voice that everyone could hear: 'Your Ireland, Sir, is all fun, no funerals; all questions and no answers.'

Here and there people whispered, lips moving angrily. The young man waited for them to stop. Someone from the front shouted back: 'Sit down or get out!'

Realising he might be shouted down he raised his voice: "Why do we leave," you ask, "what's wrong here?" you ask and "The Mountains of Mourne" which you are about to sing is indeed a comic and affecting song, but . . .'

From all over the hall people now began to murmur and mutter:

'Idiot! Sit down! Get out! Damned crackpot!'

Percy French, with upraised hands, waited for silence. Through the interruption he had smiled. Now he said, 'I'm sure you have something serious to say, Sir, but these people, God help their wit, have travelled and paid money *to hear me*.'

The hall broke out into a storm of clapping and more shouts of 'Sit down,' 'Fenian' and 'Leaguer' and 'lout'. When someone shouted: 'To hell with Parnell,' the atmosphere became suddenly unpleasant.

The interrupter stood unmoved, waiting for the

noise and abuse to stop. When it did, he waved his newspaper again, 'May I read one small item from your *Impartial Reporter*, published today Thursday, 3rd May, 1883?'

There were more shouts of 'come on' and 'we can read for ourselves'.

'Is it a long item?' Percy French asked.

'It's very short,' the young man said.

'Let's hear it then.'

The young man opened a newspaper and began:

'The heading says: "Distress in Glencolumbkille". A sub-heading: "Potatoes and meal exhausted".'

He had to wait through a hubbub of objections before he could continue:

'"Extraordinary scenes greeted our Majesty's government inspector Dr Woodhouse in the village of Glencolumbkille last weekend. Dr Woodhouse was besieged on arrival by 2,000 semi-starving people; men, women and children begging, kneeling, crying out. Visibly affected he could not make himself heard above the wailing until the Reverend Thomas Gallagher arrived to restore order."'

The two ushers were now moving from the side aisles towards where he stood. Seeing them approach, the young man said:

'Clearly, Sir, I'm not going to be permitted to read on.'

'It looks a bit like that,' Percy French said.

'Then may I say that your comic song about exile makes me unwell every time I hear it.'

From the back of the hall a voice shouted:

'Blackguard!' followed by more shouts of, 'Fenian!' 'Villain!' and 'Murderer!'

A young woman began to clap and shout support for the young man as he was led out. She was joined by other voices until gradually the audience became a cacophony of howling, shouting and clapping.

When the interrupter was gone Percy French waited for silence, looking very closely at the nails on his right hand and then on his left and all the time smiling to himself. When he said, 'Well!' there was an uneasy response. When he said, 'Well and apparently unwell,' the uneasy response became uneasy laughter. He waited for it to fade:

'If you happen to ask what's wrong in this country,' he began, 'the knife-grinders go to work. Yes, Glencolumbkille is terrible, and so is Calcutta and the Gorbals and all the poor ends of a thousand cities the world over. Today, yesterday, tomorrow, it's all heartbreaking, and all of us who live on this little island and love it probably imagine we know it well till some fine morning or evening like this, we discover suddenly that we're strangers in a strange place, where terrible things happen and you feel maybe the ship is going down. Now if you know the ship is sinking you can bail out till it goes down or you can sing funny songs. I favour the latter course. A high-falutin' "gent" in the *Irish Times* once described what I do as "a type of bucolic burlesque"; I wasn't sure if I was being commended or condemned so I went to the dictionary. It means country fun of a low kind, the opposite it would seem to city fun of a high kind. The last time I was in the Rotunda Theatre a young lad in pantaloons was singing his heart out for a lady who must have weighed in at around twenty stones. May God preserve me forever from such weighty works of art.'

Billy Winters listened fascinated as his old college comrade winked, grinned, and with gentle mockery and self-mockery, talked, clowned, sang and recited his way back into the heart of the audience. Gradually the darkness of anger was replaced by the brightness of comedy. When he ended very deliberately with 'The Mountains of Mourne' the entire hall erupted into a cheering pandemonium. It went on and on, with shouts of, 'More, more, more;' so much so that he was forced to take out a pocket-watch. He dangled it with one hand pointing at the face with his left forefinger then pointing off-stage to indicate that he had to go. Finally he left, waving, smiling like a child at an elated, enraptured, cheering audience. Minutes later his trap was at the front of the Town Hall, his wife standing on the pavement holding the door open.

Half-way to the hollow of the town, as he returned greetings from window and street, from public house and private doorway, he could still hear Miss Egerton on the piano as she accompanied most of the audience singing in loyal chorus: 'God save the Queen'.

11

The Percy French Appreciation Committee had noti-
fied in writing those notables who could, if they so
wished, avail of refreshments downstairs in the Council
Chambers after the performance. Hopefully, there they
would have an opportunity to meet and greet in person
one of the most celebrated and probably best loved
Irishmen of this or any other century. That is what the
invitation said.

Committee funds and private donations had been
given to stock the long table used for Council meetings
with a show of wines, spirits and sandwiches. Smartly
dressed staff on loan from the Royal Hotel dispensed
from plate and tray. The chamber was thrumming
warmly when Billy Winters entered. He had been down
to the lobby to see off Mickey Dolphin, warning him to
stay sober and to have Punch in the gig and the lamps
lit ready for leaving at ten o'clock. From across the
street, Alfie Gregg had waved and come over, a great
hulk of a neighbour with baggy eyes in a mournful face
still overwhelmed by the death of his son in a hunting
accident. He wanted to talk tombs and memorials. Billy
Winters had been obliged to listen, sympathise and again

hear out his grief. Twelve years ago, he, too, had suffered inconsolably, losing his wife, Cathy, and their unborn son in that terrible accident . . . 'All part, maybe,' Alfie said, 'of God's plan.' 'If that's the way it is,' Billy said, 'then God is very odd!'

Now as he crossed the high-ceilinged Council Chamber, he could see Jimmy Donnelly talking with R.I.C. Inspector Joseph Quinn. Quinn was in civilian clothes that managed the stiff look of a uniform. Billy could tell from an eye-flick less than a glance that Quinn had noted his arrival and conveyed this verbally to Jimmy Donnelly. Neither looked over. Brother officers, holy and hamfist, Mister Fairbrother's friends . . . damn little they don't know between them. All that sideways talk and silence and yet in a way they like me, trust me, and I them, I think . . . Do I? Does anyone trust anyone since the Phoenix Park? A blind, bloody island. No trust. Parnell stirring the crazy pot.

Avoiding their eyes he looked along the polished floor to where the two men stood in the centre of a group. He could see Donnelly's fine calf shoe-leather, more like dancing pumps; Cassidy's black brogues splayed out for rough work. Jig to their tune? Not me! Between them now they'll have that heckler, whoever he was, tagged, earmarked and filed for reference in Castle and Palace.

Billy Winters said 'No thank you' to a waiter proffering a tray of wine and sherry. He asked for whiskey; got it. As he began to drink and look about, he could see that the Chamber comprised two groups, one Protestant and landowning with satellite business, middle-class and professional; the other monied, and Catholic: cattle-shippers, publicans, builders, road-contractors and returnee 'millionaires' from Britain and America. Donnelly's team. He'd be touching them now or later at a meal in the parish house to keep the spires of his new Cathedral in Monaghan soaring upward, triumphant. Pathetic pride. A long way he's come from his home place, a hovel in Urbleshanny, a long way from Glencolumbkille, a long way from Christ.

Between the two groups moved free-rangers of both denominations and both genders, Garrison officers, members of ladies' guilds, town and county councillors. Where would Beth be now, had she come? With Donnelly? With me? With persons I don't know? Do I know her? Ward does now . . . Did she? With *him*! A Fenian mongrel . . . Did she? Oh God!

Someone caught his elbow gently. He turned. Gary Pringle agitated by Percy French's sudden departure. He placed his mouth close to Billy's ear:

'You know Percy's gone?'

'Yes,' Billy said, 'I knew that.'

'Should I ask for silence, tell them or . . .'

'No one seems unhappy,' Billy said, 'I'd tell them he's dodged off.'

Pringle thought about this and said:

'Yes . . . Yes . . . I believe you're right . . . Yes, I'll do that.'

Billy watched as Pringle went from group to person to couple, shaping the words, 'Bird's flown' . . . 'Yes, unfortunate . . . our guest of honour . . . did a pimpernel on us, straight out the front door and away in his gig . . . unpredictable,' and the reactions, 'Ah! what a shame' . . . 'what a pity,' . . . until someone said, 'Oh! a cute Roscommon hoor, take the money and run.'

During laughter which followed this, he saw Jimmy Donnelly extricate himself from the Catholic circle nodding here and there as he moved towards the refreshment table, a small man with sensuous lips and slow all-seeing eyes. He was wearing a trim charcoal suit cut in London or Paris, a hint of purple at the clerical collar.

'James of Clogher,' Billy said holding out his hand.

'When I was a Curate here you called me Jimmy . . . I'd still prefer that.'

The voice had acquired a kind of levitical bleat.

'I got your note,' Billy said. 'It was a help: I'm indebted,'

Donnelly gave a small shrug, waiting to hear about Fairbrother.

Instead Billy said:

'You're singing's worse than mine. I thought you people were forbidden to attend public performance?'

'Percy French *is* "a phenomenon" . . . I gave myself a dispensation.'

'Who was that heckler fella?'

'Parnell's man in Cavan . . . a chap called Thomas Leddy.'

'Which tribe?'

'Ours; non-practising. Can you tell me about Mister Fairbrother?'

For ten seconds Billy looked at the floor and then said quietly:

'It was blackmail of a sort.'

The slow eyes quickened and rolled away as the pursed lips said:

'I suppose I can't ask?'

'No,' Billy said, 'you can't.'

Donnelly's face did not respond. The colour of his voice became a degree colder as he said:

'I inquired because possibly I can help.'

Who, Billy thought, does he think he is that he can help me. He looked away until the silence obliged Donnelly to say:

'I hope you didn't concede?'

'I gave him my boot,' Billy said, 'almost.'

'Good for you.'

Billy Winters then inclined his head towards Jimmy Donnelly's teacup.

'What's that brown stuff?'

Donnelly made a chalice offering of his teacup and said:

'Tea; Bewley's most likely, and very good.'

'How in hell do you people keep on the straight and narrow?' Billy asked. 'Or do you?'

Turning crude now . . . must be drunker than he looks. Two hundred years of church-building to catch up on, meantime their wretched hymns and barren services in our stolen sanctuaries, hunted from rock to rock, castration once proposed for all Irish priests in their mother of parliaments; use us, despise us, fear and hate us still. Donnelly cleared his throat:

'I've a Cathedral to finish: *that's* putting money in *your* purse, Billy, *and* there's pastoral work, when I'm not begging funds, *and* I read and travel a lot *and* I sing betimes, poorly as you remarked . . . all that keeps me half-decent for whatever judgement's pending.'

Billy Winters again signalled to a passing boy waiter, quaffed the remainder of his glass; took another whiskey from the proffered tray. The boy added water, smiling respectfully towards the Bishop of Clogher who returned the smile. Young Coogan . . . is it? . . . very like, or kin, I'd swear. 'Cultra', that white Negro look, wide nose and full mouth, a bit tinkerish, attractive though. Billy's hand on his arm saying something, must know him, knows everyone. What's on Fairbrother's file? Some indiscretion? Farm boys? Caesar's complaint?

Hardly. Too much of a ladies' man. Lad's embarrassed now, I'm staring too hard . . . look away.

Jimmy Donnelly looked up at the ceiling and drank a mouthful of tea.

Dull, bare, municipal ceiling, a far cry from Easter in the Sistine: Pope's Mass, choir singing Allegri's 'Miserere', that boy tenor. Dear God, the overwhelming beauty. Can such wonders be and no God? how grand heaven, after all, meeting dear Mama again. And poor poor Father boxed a month today, dead and buried in Urbleshanny. Wept both sides at the end, so sorrowful even now to remember. Dear God, have pity on John Joseph Donnelly: forgive him his sins, Lord Jesus Christ have mercy on his soul; have mercy on us all.

For an instant Jimmy Donnelly could feel his eyes swimming. He blinked vigorously to disperse the tears. The boy waiter had moved on and Billy Winters turned as an Anglo-Irish voice obtruded confidently:

'He was one of Parnell's cronies.' The voice dropped to a loud conspiratorial whisper intended for overhearing:

'And if what's circulating is even half-true, he'll drown in the same bog as he drowned Boycott and God knows how many others.'

Then a woman's voice; American:

'Our press over there described Mister Parnell as "a sleek Irish dude".'

Again the Anglo voice asking:

'How should we spell that, dear – with or without an "e"?'

Restrained laughter.

The Bishop of Clogher glanced towards the voices. Anglo rule-of-thumb. If it's Ireland or Irish, mock it instantly. Guilt. Nothing to envy in that pagan island but Shakespeare, and Parnell no dud for their mockery

... on everyone's lips. That proud eagle face ... contemptuous of their commons and common morality. Shameful duplicity with O'Shea's wife ... his ruination if true ... and ours. Tim Healy swears he's an Atheist ... Our first President? Atheist? Unthinkable.

Billy Winters was at his side again, a full glass of whiskey in his hand. This time James of Clogher inclined his head towards Billy's glass:

'*That's* beginning to show.'

'Drunk my Lord, and for good cause.'

'Can I share it?'

'You just did ... Percy the peacemaker. That was the best evening ever in this town.'

'Yes, of course ... The man has something genial and extraordinary ... and he's a great deal shrewder than the stuff he writes.'

'Stuff?'

'The, eh, it's doggerel Billy ... Albeit charming, but doggerel nonetheless.'

'You're as grand as Beth Winters. I thought he was wonderful.'

'Where's your gig stabled?'

'At the Royal.'

'I'm going that way now. There's an item or two I want to talk about if you'd like to walk with me.'

'Why not.'

'I'll have to make my excuses; back presently.'

The Bishop of Clogher squeezed his elbow amicably and began padding about the room pausing briefly. Billy could see him saying: 'Yes of course', 'Yes, I'll do that', 'I'd love to'; a quick word here, a smile there, the left hand promptly extended for kissing, the right hand touching a face or chignon, a purblind nod towards the Protestant circle where some watched, half-curious, others with simulated blindness.

Billy Winters watched them watching the Bishop of Clogher. Cheeky, smooth little bugger ticking me off like that. Doesn't need whiskey; intoxicated with himself. This room packed with Tammany Taigs, vindictive unforgiving pack, outbreed us yet, that's what they're up to, get the land back, get us off it or bury us in it, convert us or kill us, burning zeal . . . Still got half a notion he'll make a convert of me . . . no bloody fear, Sir, *not* my soul . . . *not* my land, *not* my gold, defend it to the death. *Items*! . . . what items? . . . what's he after? . . . Parnell's fornications? Fairbrother's quest? Beth? He knows it all, oldest secret service in the world, teach intrigue to intriguers, unholy office, bad lot at the back of it. Cathy always running to confession, forever quoting him, her Curate then; Father Jimmy this, Father Jimmy that, Father Jimmy the other, sickening dose, tattle tattle tattle, in a box, all breathless, telling tales out of bed, tail-end stuff mostly they hear, in half-dark whispered, pushing for low details:

'Down there, child?'

'Yes, Father.'

'And did you?'

'Yes, Father.'

'Down there, child?'

'Yes, Father.'

'And will you promise me?'

'Father, yes, Father, Father.'

'Go in peace, my child.' Childless all of them. Or was she making it all up to tease me . . . mocking Donnelly . . . mocking me . . . Sly shepherds they are . . . scare the flock to keep their grip . . . Rome's crooked crozier.

But soft you . . . Here he comes! Wee Jimmy; Rome's Lord of Clogher, not mine.

His farewells complete, the Bishop of Clogher saw, from the centre of the Council Chamber, the glazed stare of drunkness staring back. Oh dear. Oh dear me! Foolish unstable man. Make some excuse, get off without him. Hate drunken gibberish. Can I give him the slip? Dear God, he's following me. Over his shoulder the Bishop said, 'Maybe you'd care to stay on, Billy?'

'No, my time is up,' Billy said.

Donnelly was tempted to an obvious response. He waited for the comparative anonymity of the Diamond where he stood in the centre of the street looking down into the crown of his topper which he held with both hands, aware of candle-lit windows, of people watching from doorways, of a high, clear moon glinting on rooflights:

'You mentioned items,' Billy said.

'Keep your voice down. Yes . . . The Parnell affair is on all our minds, very much . . . he stayed with you, Billy; quite an honour. How did you find him?'

'Very strange,' Billy said. 'Small wonder he went bankrupt. All mad as hatters, the Parnells; well-suited to running this mad bloody country.'

The Bishop smiled curiously and said, 'Nothing political?'

'*One* word. I asked him about the "invincibles", the hangings, the crowds kneeling night and day outside Kilmainham saying rosaries for young Brady . . . He muttered one word I couldn't catch . . . Beth heard it . . . "Scum".'

It was almost as if Donnelly hadn't heard, as he said: 'I haven't seen Elizabeth for a year. I wanted to ask closely about her and of course about your good self.'

My bad self and goody Beth his ward. Sees *himself*, Billy thought, as her guardian. Poor child, a lost soul in a blighted house. Does he know about the other Ward, my tenant, the Fenian knife-smuggler, her invincible lover?

'You don't want to talk *with* me,' Billy said, 'you want information *from* me.'

Donnelly's smile became forced. He turned, began to walk away. Ridiculous man: blunt, coarse, Ulster and proud of it. Crossing the Diamond, two soldiers with Cockney voices saluted the cloaked clergymen holding a topper. Donnelly returned their salute with a nod, and muttered:

'Gentlemen.'

Billy Winters responded with an expansive salute:

'Legionnaires from Putney, I'd say.'

Both watched as the soldiers went into a public house.

'Mr Parnell is right about *them*: there can be no peace here till they're gone.'

'Them,' Billy said.

He repeated the word loudly, 'Them . . . That's me, Sir, my people. "Them" is me, Billy Winters, and if they go, what happens? I want no truck with your Infallible Man in Rome . . . none.'

Donnelly glanced away for a moment. Far too drunk now to bother with. Move away after this; sanctuary: the parish house. He heard himself say:

'It's almost three hundred years now, Billy; six generations, *that's* how long you've been with us, how long more before you become part of us . . . three hundred more?'

'Never,' Billy said.

'A pity . . . a great pity you feel that way.'

This time the Bishop walked away without looking back. He kept walking into the dark, as the drunken voice called after him:

'Being born in a stable doesn't make you a horse, that's what the Duke of Wellington said about being born here.'

From the half-light of the hollow Donnelly's voice came back:

'It could also make you a God. He rules the universe!'

'A bloody bad job he made of this wee corner,' Billy muttered, as he flung a dismissive arm towards the hollow and the neat footsteps tapping away into silence. Blind to watchers in doorways, to the high clear moon and stars, Billy Winters felt suddenly alien, angry and alone as he headed down Town Hall Street towards the yard and stables of the Imperial Hotel.

12

Mercy had packed her own and Gerry's few belongings into two hessian bags. McCafferty's pony and trap had called to collect. When Beth had asked why Gerry had to go, Mercy seemed evasive, almost angry:

'He can't manage on his own.'

'Why not?'

'He's no wit: you won't be here; I won't be here; he can't mind himself.'

Her mood had stayed the same until they were parting at the back door where they embraced. Both wept. The suddenness and strangeness of this departure left Beth feeling deeply unhappy. She went up to the fountain hill and sat in the fort looking down at the Lower Lough and out to Corvey Island, watching the slow twilight merge into dusk. For the last time?

In the half-light of that first dawn with Ward when she had said: 'You were never out of my head from that time we met in the yard,' he hadn't replied. She had asked: 'Was it like that with you?' The silence went on so long she got up on her elbow. Ward was deep asleep. The effect of that half minute's silence was so unnerving that she was careful thereafter to ask questions and say things with more circumspection:

'I love you more than life, but then I'm not sure what I think about life.'

His response to that had been:

'It's a gamble.'

'And does the stealing not worry you?' He seemed not to have heard.

'Surely it must?'

'It's not stealing,' he had said, 'it's taking back what was stole from us long ago.'

Before she could comment on this, he had asked:

'How often does he go to that safe?'

'Not often.'

'How often is that?'

'I don't know, hardly ever maybe.'

'All we need is two days and we're away with it.'

It was dark in the house when she got back. She went to the hanging cupboard in the scullery, and took out a black lacquered box the size of a shoebox. It contained bandages, scissors, glass jars, gentian violet, iodine, and a small envelope Ward had given her containing four bromide tablets. On the outside it said FOR ANIMAL USE ONLY. She put the four tablets in a mortar bowl, ground them down with a pestle, scooped half the powder into a small glazed jug, poured in water and watched the powder dissolve. She put in her forefinger and tasted it. It had a faintly sour flavour. She then made cold bacon sandwiches, mixed the rest of the powder with mustard and spread it on the buttered bread. She carried the sandwiches on a plate to the dining-room table, aware all the time of her beating heart and a slight shake in her hand.

A fire in the bedroom grate had burned low as she sat watching the window, waiting, half-listening, re-reading *Nicholas Nickleby*, trying to make sense of words on the page. 'They walked upon the rim of the devil's punch-bowl; and Smike listened with greedy interest as Nicholas read the inscription upon the stone, reared upon that wild spot.' Old Nick, young Nick, that convent by a lake long ago in Monaghan Town talking about banshees, ghosts and devils with Connie Ryan next to her in the dormitory. Connie lived on a farm opposite the Devil's Bite in Tipperary, a great gap in the mountains. At the start of every term she was so homesick she cried herself to sleep pining for her own fields. She, Beth, would be leaving forever the miraculous skies of Fermanagh and, Oh God, she thought . . . this place, these fields: in May? The standing stone, the five limes, the fountain hill, the long field, the fort field, the bog field, the lake field and the lough itself and Corvey Island and the myriad memories of growing up here . . . the only world she understood or cared about . . . Leaving? . . . never to return? . . . never? . . . and this morning she had stumbled out in half-light to save a bloated cow! . . . What matter one cow in God's ledger or the devil's? . . . What matter if the whole herd had perished . . . God, she thought yet again, would not smile gently on what was planned for tonight.

Outside, under a cold moon, she now heard from a long way off the sound of iron hooves, the squeal of an axle or gig springs, the rattle of wheels on the avenue. Billy Winters seemed to be singing contrapuntally to a melody from Mickey Dolphin's mouth organ.

Already her heart had begun to stumble unevenly, straightened, and now quickened to beat in a way that made her breathe deeply. She picked up the paraffin lamp, brought it down to the dining-room, lit a candle in the scullery and kitchen and went up to the long window at the turn of the staircase looking down on the yard. In the moonlight, the old labrador came out stiffly to greet the returning concert-goers.

Mickey Dolphin had began unstrapping the gig. He wheeled it into the coach house and had come back now to take the collar and britchen off Punch. Billy stood watching. She then heard him address the horse, as Mickey led him to a paddock behind the yard.

'Above all beasts I bow to you, Lord of all.'

He then stood in the middle of the yard staring up at the moon. He continued doing this for what seemed like five minutes or longer. She could hear a corncrake in the distance and the bleat of sheep over by Brackagh. Mickey Dolphin came back to the yard. For a while they stood talking, then Mickey left for the loft bedroom over the coach house. Sound of the back-door latch, the bolt thumping into its holder, footsteps on the scullery flags, then on the pine boards of the kitchen floor.

Upstairs in her bedroom she sat on trying to read till she heard the rattle of keys in the dining-room. She closed the novel, waiting. There was a sound of the sideboard cupboard opening, the clink of glass against a bottle as Billy Winters moved towards the dining-room table. She would not have to suggest a nightcap. She stood, picked up a lamp, took a very deep breath and went downstairs and straight into the dining-room. He pointed an angry finger at her as she came in:

'You missed it, girl, the best night ever in the town of Enniskillen; you might say the best night ever in the province of Ulster and you out here on your own with Mr Keats.'

She could not tell if he was half, three quarters or fully drunk. Certainly he was not swaying, and as he spoke the words were not obviously slurred: 'Is there a splash of spring water?' She went immediately to the scullery, picked up the jug spiked with bromide, and brought it back to the table where he was muttering to himself about water-rights, grist-mills, flax-mills and water-mills. 'It's the spring water I'm after,' he said. As she put the jug down he said:

'They march along the deep, and that's where I'd keep them . . . down on the ocean floor!'

'Yes, Sir.'

'Bewley's brew . . . judgements pending!'

He began laughing, spluttering. When this subsided she said:

'I can make you a pot of tea.'

'No tea, none of the brown stuff, no, I'll stay *loyal* to my own pure spring water.' He winked.

She watched him put out his hand again for the water jug. It was like watching something in a dream. She noticed a welt from a deep cut and the way the skin tensed and smoothed as he poured. As he began to talk she sat at the table watching the water. It did not discolour or cloud the whiskey. She felt her mouth go dry as he talked, half-hearing:

'Town Hall was packed to the gills with high, middle and low gentry, the blind earl and that fella from Crom with his heiress, the American bride, and the Wrights and the Millers and the Mooreheads, and old Leslie from Glaslough in his kilt and monocle, and Hare-Foster who was always prancing round your mother . . . and your fat friend at school . . . what's her name? . . . Pig-packer's daughter . . .' 'Roisin . . . Roisin Reilly,' Beth said.

'The very girl . . . and two Bishops . . . ours and

yours. Your wee fella Donnelly had his chain gang with him. Maguires, and liars and small squires and dodgy contractors and cattle-shippers along with the "millionaire" Micks and Chicago brogues, all there to hear our Percy . . . And because he was an hour late your wee Jimmy sang for us.'

Billy now suddenly burst into 'Kathleen Mavoorneen', sang a verse, glanced at Beth, and said:

'And of course myself, William Hudson Winters *without* his daughter Elizabeth . . . And when Wee Jimmy was done singing and everyone was moved to embarrassment or tears, I wondered would Christ have sung arias in the back garden of Latlurcan House in Monaghan Town. Would he have travelled incognito to operas at Milan . . . or Rome, shipped home paintings from Paris? All the while caning pennies from half-starved paupers to build a brute Cathedral . . . Yes, I did wonder . . . He'll not go to Glencolumbkille for his holidays, Wee Jimmy. One of Parnell's cronies tried to foul things up. Percy was fit for him, and at the end we were all singing with him and clapping.'

It was clear now to Beth that he was oddly drunk. He had paused to take a mouthful of whiskey and her heart twisted now as she saw him lick his upper lip. He did not say anything, look at the glass or smell it:

'Everyone stood and for that minute we were *one*: everyone on that second floor in the Town Hall of Enniskillen, all of us: *one*; you missed it, girl . . . badly.'

And because she thought he would see the beating of her heart through her blouse she made herself say:

'Perhaps I did.' There was a pause. As he sat looking at the whiskey in the glass, she asked, 'Did you get talking to him afterwards, to Mr French?'

'No, he was booked, away, out the door; no one got talking to him, but I'll tell you one thing, he's worth a whole gang of Parnell's trouble-makers, bloody dividers! Percy made *one* of us tonight: he's a magician!'

Beth was so transfixed as she watched him lift the glass of whiskey to his mouth again that she asked without wanting to know:

'And did you get talking to Mr Fairbrother?'

'Yes, I talked with Mr Fairbrother.'

Billy Winters stared so long at the table that she thought perhaps he had lost track of what he was saying. Then his gaze shifted. He looked from her forehead to her tranquil eyes, to her brown hair, to the fullness of her mouth, to the line of her neck, then back to the eyes that looked straight into his:

'Green and orange and foul and fair, is what Mr Fairbrother seems to think of Ireland and her people. "Yes, Sir," he said, "the bogs of Ireland are full of secrets and Christ alone knows what goes on in the bogs of Ireland." That was mostly what he talked about . . . secrets.'

Beth waited for him to continue. There was about his drunkenness now the sway and danger of a wounded animal as he pointed directly at her and said:

'He knows a thing or two, the fairest of us all . . . Parnell's philandering with O'Shea's wife, all that. When Jimmy Donnelly knows *that* for certain he'll sing solemn requiems all round . . . and farewell Parnell!'

Billy Winters took a bite from a sandwich and wrinkled up his nose:

'By God, you fairly lashed on the mustard, girl.'

'I know you're partial to it, Sir.'

'He asked about you.'

'Who did, Sir?'

'Mr Fairbrother ... *What*, I asked him, do decent Irish girls get up to in Italy or elsewhere? It's not smuggling guns or dynamite. It's minding children, I said, governessing with an old family near Pompeii! ... De Cortese. Like her mother, I said, a governess well fit to govern ... Then *what*, he wanted to know, had brought you home? My increasing age, I told him ... *loyalty* perhaps to the modest house of Winters, to the fair fields of Fermanagh ... *not* the ties of kith and kin ... that would be a falsehood and on your behalf I would not *deceive* Mr Fairbrother ... No, no, so I said ... hearth and home, Sir ... be certain she's had no truck with Mr Garibaldi or his cut-throat Corsican Fenians ... a decent girl, I said, of pure and honest disposition, hard-working, bright, trustworthy.' Billy stared away for a moment at the rectangle of moon on the carpet and pitchpine surround and said almost casually:

'I didn't mention that you'd curtsied to Mr Parnell here in the hall ... I wouldn't let you down that way.'

Stung to sudden anger she said:

'I did *not* curtsy to Mr Parnell!'

'I was here, I saw you ... you curtsied to a Protestant Wicklow landlord.'

'I inclined my head, Sir.'

'You curtsied! ... I wouldn't mind Mercy falling on her knees to kiss his hand ... they all do that here ... kiss your hand, cut your throat ... all the one ... but you, Beth ... you're proud as your mother ... proud as hell, and you curtsied.'

She was glad of the unexpected and real anger which helped mask the tremor in her hands, the painful beating of her heart.

Billy went on:

'Percy's the man for me, Percy the peacemaker; he deserves a curtsy or two . . . Percy is *my* hero.'

As she watched him lift the glass of whiskey to his mouth, she heard herself say almost without thinking:

'They often end as clowns or criminals.'

Billy looked at her.

'Who do?'

'Heroes, Sir.'

'The greatest Irishman of this century or any other! A clown? . . . a criminal? . . . just who in hell do *you* think *you* are girl?'

'*You* can tell *me* that, Sir.'

'What do you mean?' For half a minute she said nothing, then calmly and quietly said:

'You know what I mean . . . My real father.'

'You're being impertinent!'

'No, Sir, pertinent.'

She could see that she had reined his glowing account of Percy French in the Town Hall to a sudden jolting halt:

'A simple question begs a simple answer.'

'You ask that *tonight* above all nights!'

He blinked, put down the whiskey glass, and looked at her.

Silence but for the ticking of the hall-clock. Finally Billy muttered:

'Hawk-proud and wren-poor . . . the dodgy daughter of a dodgy horseman!' He then looked at Beth and said carefully:

'Twenty-five years ago I made a solemn covenant with the Roman Catholic Church that all children born to us would be of that faith . . . a small matter I thought . . . I'd no faith much to lose, I'll grant you I was no saint . . . and gold can put a halo on the devil . . . but to marry as *she* did, knowing what she *knew* . . . no giddy mishap or drunken blunder . . . no, no . . . coldly, deliberately . . . monstrously . . . duped me, and I loved her! . . . my Jezebel ripped by a mad bull . . . I loved her.'

He began to tremble, covered his face with both hands, giving great inward gulps. As the trembling increased, his hands gouged into his face. There was no further sound. When she could see the tears coming through his fingers, the effect was so grotesque, so unexpected that she found tears coming down her own immobile cheeks. As she put out her hand to touch his arm, he uncovered his face and shouted suddenly:

'A brazen, bare-faced bitch! You ask now and I did then . . . asked and asked and asked till she screamed up in my face that she didn't know . . . It could, she screamed, be "One of two" . . . That she loved neither, "a bit of bad luck" . . . The Corrys . . . father and son deflowered and dowered, bull calf and Scrub Island . . . I gave you nothing but your name . . . Elizabeth . . . that much I was allowed.'

He was shaking a little. As he lifted the glass some of it splashed on the table, '"One of two; a bit of bad luck," that's your answer.' Beth got up went to the scullery where she stood wringing out a cloth at the sink till she heard Billy's voice coming from the dining-room:

'Come in here, Beth: sit by me, girl, I'm not out to hurt, to pass on any cup of sorrow, bowl of poison, not a thimbleful of tears would I wish on you child for all your days . . . how you came into the world is not your doing . . . truth is you're all I care about in the world now.'

She knew from other nights that it was simpler to pretend to go along with him. She returned to the dining-room. After a staring silence he put his hand on her shoulder and said:

172

'My crime, girl, is I reared you and loved you over-much; the best of men can make the worst of blunders and be heart-sorry ... and the best of women ... I suppose.'

Unpredictably he stood suddenly, knocking over a chair. He glanced at her and said:

'I'll tell you more,' he paused, then said: 'No, *I've* told enough ... *you* tell *me* now.'

'Tell, Sir?'

'Yes: tell!'

Silence, till Billy Winters asked:

'Nothing?'

'What is there to tell, Sir, except you must be very tired ... You should be in your bed!'

He finished the glass of whiskey, put it down on the table and moved towards the door. She moved back to let him pass, listening with all her body as she heard him stumble. She counted up to twenty, waiting for him to move. Silence. She then went to the dining-room doorway. He was sitting on the second step of the staircase staring at the pine boards of the hall floor. He did not look up. She did not speak, was startled when he did:

'What are you staring at?'

'I heard you stumble, Sir.'

'Has the old codger broken his back, his skull, his neck.'

He pressed his head against the banister rails and muttered:

'Are you honest, girl? Would you deceive me?'

'How could I, Sir.'

'You tell me ... Can you, will you, should you, ought you? Could you pretend I'm your confessor? Or are you loyal to Rome like your mother?'

'Rome is as much to me, Sir, as your bowler hat is to you.'

'And that's what?'

'Dressing up to keep others down.'

Billy snuffed out a laugh as he said:

'By God, you're crafty: you have the answers.'

'Do I, Sir?'

'Your mother's daughter; that's for certain!'

He glanced at her again and levered himself to his feet. She watched him as he used the banisters to pull himself up, step by step, to the upper landing where he turned and said:

'You'll lock up, girl?'

'Of course I will, Sir . . . Good night!'

For a moment he stood pointing down at her about to say something, changed his mind and crossed the landing without mishap or stumble to his bedroom. For five minutes she stood in the doorway of the lower hall listening. She could tell from the creak of certain boards that he was either in bed or sitting on his bed. She went back into the dining-room, picked up the fallen chair, placed it at the table and sat. The carriage-clock on the mantelpiece told her it was a quarter to one. No light for at least four hours.

At one o'clock, she picked up a paraffin lamp and went up to Billy Winters' bedroom. He was lying sideways across the bed, one arm tucked awkwardly under his body, one booted foot cocked out, the other on the bed. She loosened his collar, undid his laces, pulled off his boots, turned him on his side and put a pillow under his head.

During this she was watching the gold chain with the keys lock-snapped onto a specially tailored leather loop above his left-hand pocket. Twice she tried to undo the lock-snap. It was too tight, her fingers fumbling at the patent safety catch. She crossed to her bedroom, returned with scissors, cut the leather loop and pulled the chain slowly from the pocket till the bunch of keys appeared on Billy Winters' hip. Her hands closed round them. She put them in her skirt pocket, covered him with an eiderdown, crossed to her bedroom for the empty case under her bed and went down to the dining-room.

She placed the lamp on the floor and knelt, going through the keys, her hands trembling. The key of the panel door was simple to guess. It opened easily, then the steel door sliding sideways, then the double-sided brass key and the safe swung open silently. She pulled out the drawer containing the gold. She began filling handfuls of gold coins into stockings, knotting each stocking at the top and placing it in the case. In less than half an hour, she had emptied the steel drawer. She paused once as Billy groaned upstairs. When she had snapped the case closed, she began to look through other shelves and boxes in the safe: bric-à-brac, personal details and possessions of generations, a request from Henry Grattan for money, the thank-you letter from Parnell, deeds of transfer, bundles of diaries, rent books, agreements, share certificates of a South African diamond mine.

In a small rosewood box, she found a wedding ring, a lady's pocket-watch and an envelope containing two faded photographs of her mother and Billy. One was taken in a studio: both standing looking directly at the camera. The other was taken outside, with her mother seated, her hair tied up, and Billy standing behind her, his hands on her shoulders. Billy was smiling; her mother looked ghostly. In another envelope, she saw WILL: COPY. It was dated July 1880. She opened it and read. Through the fustian language it was clear that she, Beth Winters, if she married, must marry a man of the Protestant faith. Failing that, all land, monies and shares would remain in trust. If she proved childless, the entire estate would pass to the next of kin. There then followed a list of names of people that she had scarcely ever heard of, most of them from County Tyrone. She took out the three-cornered beaver cap, placed the will inside it and heard herself say:

'If I'm a thief, you're a cheat, Sir! It must be bred in both of us.'

She brought the case of gold to the scullery, went upstairs, collected her other case from under the bed and brought it near the back door. It would be three hours before light. She lay down, very wide awake, on the long upright couch between the two windows in the kitchen. She closed her eyes, certain she would not sleep. She could try to rest and maybe the painful gnawing at her heart would ease, because all the time something kept saying to her: I can stop this now, I can put it back, lock the safe, return the keys and leave tomorrow . . . without the gold.

Soon, she thought, light would come flooding into the yard and kitchen of Clonoula, into the dirt streets and gardens, the towns and villages and town lands of Fermanagh, into the fields, the watery acres of Lough Erne flowing onwards to the Atlantic where they would sail away to a new world. And she would never again hear Billy's drunken voice singing 'Love thee dearest, love thee'. And as she tried to block off the sound of his voice she saw the red-headed dwarf in the wattle house, then he was sitting high in the swing tree pointing down and chanting and shrieking 'Jezebel, Jezebel, Jezebel'. It was her mother on the swing. As she fell to the ground, a pack of hounds attacked, pulling and tearing and ripping. Then the dwarf was laughing and throwing gold coins into the briars and nettles of the secret garden, and she was sitting up awake, frightened, her heart thumping. She looked at the clock. She had been asleep scarcely five minutes. She got up again. Sleep was more unnerving than staying awake. She went out to the hall and stood listening to the hollow ticking of the clock and, from the open door of the upper landing, the steady rhythm of Billy Winters' breathing.

Back in the kitchen she tried to read. Again and again she had to re-read sentences. She could not disconnect her mind from the action just taken. It would be simpler to deal with what was in her head by trying some way to explain in a letter. She sat down at the kitchen table, and for almost two hours she wrote and re-wrote, tore up and started again. Finally she finished a letter which she left on the table:

Clonoula
4th May 1883
The kitchen 3:30 a.m.

Dear Billy, Sir,
   What I have done and the manner of my leaving will I know enrage you. I am sorry. You left me little choice.
 How you have behaved with me this past three years, you know full well, though every now and then you pretend to innocence. In your own words I had:
 'A roof over my head, the run of my teeth and a fair allowance. What more could any woman want?'

*The little guilt I felt vanished when I read
the terms of your will. The 'love' you sometimes
profess for me and have willed for me is more
fear and hatred of the people you have used and
despised for so long.*

*Against all common sense, I have in a way
always loved you and still do, in a way, and will
miss this house where I was born and the fields
where I grew up . . . for the most part happily.*

I remain or more correctly I should say I leave,

*Yours sincerely,
Beth 'one of two'*

She tore the sheet from the notebook and left it on the
kitchen table, opened the back door quietly, carried the
two cases out, left them on the sandstone flag of the
doorstep and then pulled the door to, dropping the
latch soundlessly into its holder. As she crossed the
moonlit cobbles, a vixen shrieked up by the ravine. It
was answered by the old labrador barking defensively
somewhere at the front of the house. She walked out
under the arch, placed the two cases in a small, rarely
used dog-cart up-ended in a lean-to off the back lane.
She then went into the garden paddock with a handful
of crushed oats in a bucket. Punch, lying under a beech
tree, got up and snorted, a graceful apparition in silver
as he walked towards her. He followed the bucket to the
lean-to. She let him feed as she harnessed, bridled and
placed him in the shafts of the dog-cart, methodically
buckling, strapping and tightening chains to the collar
and britchen.

She then led him through the trunks of rearing beech
on the back lane. Above them, the first hint of blood in

the east as the outbuildings of the yards fell away, a grey stillness in the fields on either side as she approached the main avenue, tense, listening out for Ward to call or whistle.

It was Punch who alerted her before she heard anything. She could feel a vibration from the reins. He stopped, suddenly trembling all over, as she asked:

'What are you afraid of, Punch? Don't be silly!'

Now startled herself, she began stroking his neck, talking quietly saying 'it's all right, it's all right', staring ahead into the half-light, listening. When she heard the sounds she knew exactly what it was and said aloud:

'It's all right Punch, it's only the Dummy McGonnell, it's only the Dummy.'

When the Dummy came into view, he was mouthing and grimacing, strange squealy noises coming from his larynx. When she could see him properly in the moonlight, he stood very still, staring at her almost with disbelief. He then turned towards the thirty-acre scrub alongside the avenue, brandishing his stick, waving it with mock heroic threat over his head, a gesture she had seen him use before in response to mockery or refusal of alms. What could have made him so angry, in the middle of the avenue at four o'clock in the morning? Surely Liam had kept well out of his way?

He now began walking towards her, looking round and pointing all the time and when she saw him closer, his eyes were huge. The nasal whining was almost like the whinnying of a horse. He kept pointing back towards the scrub. Without attempting to lip-read her 'what's wrong', he took the reins from her hands, gripped her arm with the other hand and kept walking, turning Punch and the dog-cart and heading back up the side avenue towards the yard and going so quickly that the dog-cart wheel went up on the side of the ditch almost coping. Clearly he must have seen or heard Liam Ward in the trees and been frightened. There was no point in trying to resist or argue. When they reached the yard he seemed if anything more frenetic, pushing her towards the door and pointing back all the time.

He sat down at the kitchen table, his great bald head and jowls gleaming with sweat. He kept mouthing, showing his black rotting teeth in red gums, his lips making incomprehensible movements. Aware that she could not understand, he began sign language, trying to make her see what he had seen. Suddenly impatient, he gestured for a pencil and paper, for milk and bread. When he picked up the letter she had written to Billy Winters, she took it from him, put it on the dresser, and placed the notebook and pencil down in front of him. She then put her forefinger to her lips and pointed upstairs indicating that Billy Winters was asleep and he must be quiet. She went out to the hall and listened. Steady breathing as before, this time combined with a snoring sound.

When she came back to the kitchen, the Dummy was scribbling and drawing. He looked up for a moment, pushing the notebook towards her. He pointed at a chair indicating that she should sit beside him, stuffed a half-slice of bread into his mouth, gulped at the mug of milk and began pointing with a black-nailed forefinger at what he had drawn. For a minute or longer, she looked at it. She could make no sense of it. Then gradually something alerted her as he insisted almost angrily that she follow line by line what he had sketched. She realised now that she would get away if she really paid attention to what had frightened him. He had established on paper the house, the yard, the front, the main avenue, the side avenue and the thirty acres of scrub. He had then pencilled in the short cut from the main avenue to the county road, then mime by mime with dummy language and mouthing he conveyed to her that he was asleep in the darkness of the scrub. He asked her did she understand. Yes, she nodded, she understood. In the laurels? Yes, she understood, and nodded again. He was asleep? Yes she understood. Something woke him. He saw by the the light of a lantern two men with spades, a rope and some kind of hammer. It had a spike. She questioned him saying 'one man'. He shook his head vigorously to convey 'no' . . . *two* men . . . and the two men he said were digging beside a dead ash tree. It was very overgrown, difficult to approach but he crawled to where he could see them properly. Her mind had now moved from impatient attention to sudden and extraordinary alertness. Why, how, would the Dummy invent such incredible detail? Who were these men? What were they digging for? She pointed at the sketch and asked why they were digging. The Dummy lip-read and then drew a rectangular box on a separate sheet. On the box he put a cross. Underneath the box he drew another rectangle, pointed at it. When she said the word 'grave' he nodded, blessed himself, pointed at her and drew his long forefinger across his throat, pointing at her with his other forefinger.

Her heart had already slowed as the details emerged: the rope, the spiked hammer, the digging. Now she mimed to find out what the two men looked like. As he began to sketch on a fresh piece of paper, she knew what she would see before it was drawn, Ward's profile, a foxy effect, stressing the nose. Spiky hair and two circles for eyes conveyed Blinky Blessing, and as he drew a narrow face she could feel the colour draining from her own, could see her hands whitening on the table and then the burning of tears down the coldness of her cheeks as the room moved into an underwater blur of rage.

It was the Dummy's grip that kept her from falling off the chair. As normality returned, she covered her face, aware of a screaming noise in her throat, a sort of discordant viol to the Dummy's rumbling bass. This seemed to go on for quite a while. She was aware that her eyes and her nose were running. She got up, blew her nose, composed herself, looked at the Dummy and pointed again at what he had drawn asking with her mouth '*my* grave'. He nodded, very slowly, opening his hands almost apologetically and shaking his head slowly.

She had no reason whatsoever to disbelieve him. He was regarded as a rogue of sorts, but why would he invent such a tale? Yet it must be some kind of mistake, some kind of illusion or nightmare. Perhaps he had imagined it all. There was nothing to suggest that he was lying and she could see that he was frightened by what he had seen. She would have to find this grave herself, look down into it – the place where she would be butchered and buried by two men, one of them her lover whose child she carried. It seemed to her that nothing in the world could be more brutal, unbelievable or grotesque.

She now mimed to him that he would have to take her and show her exactly where this grave had been dug. With nasal whining and much head-shaking, he made it clear that he would not. She mimed that he had nothing to fear. He continued to refuse. Of course, he was afraid. He did not know that there was a ransom of gold in a suitcase in the dog-cart outside and that for this, men would kill. Without the gold she or the Dummy were no more likely to be killed than any other human under the moon. More and more she began to grasp the coldness, the callousness, the calculation.

She picked up the Dummy's caricature, looking at it closely as if it could, in some way, offer an explanation. There was nothing to explain beyond the fact that it was a simple brutal plot. She would disappear, likewise the gold. They would look for her here, in Britain and America. They would never find her, nor the gold. It was safe. Both were safe. They had planned the perfect theft, the perfect murder. Nothing could go wrong. Disbelief now altered to an anger so intense it caused her to tremble. She could see that the Dummy now imagined she was trembling with fear. He put up his fists towards the door much as to say 'don't be afraid, I'm here'. She muttered and turned away lest he could lip-read, saying aloud 'It's not my blood they're after, it's Billy Winters' gold.' She now turned towards the Dummy and said:

'If Billy Winters wakens we'll be in trouble. He'll come down here and put you to clearing ditches, gathering stones.'

He growled and frowned, pointing with a thumb towards his back.

'I know about your bad back . . . You'd better move out now . . . you can sleep in a loft in the lower yard, go on now, and thank you for warning me: you've saved my life.'

She could see that he was puzzled by her matter-of-factness. She held the door. As he was crossing the yard she became aware of encroaching light. She untied the leather cases, carried them into the living-room and began emptying the gold back into the tray of the safe, aware that it was taking much less time than the stuffing of coins into stockings, but half-aware also that it was noisier. She was so engrossed with this unloading that only part of her realised that she was crying. Her nose was blocked again. As she reached for her pocket handkerchief she became aware of a sudden change of light, of a consciousness of something. Outside in the half-light, there was a sudden thrum of pigeon wings.

She continued to unload, and then knew that what she could hear was breathing. She turned, startled, expecting to see the Dummy standing in the doorway. It was Billy Winters and never in her life had she seen on his or any human face such a naked expression of shock, disbelief and hatred. She opened her mouth to speak, to explain. It was a scream that emerged as he came rolling towards her with extraordinary speed and agility, attacking her like a windmill, one whirling foot smashing her arm and scattering the suitcase and the coins, then the talon-grip of his left hand, while his right fist smashed her face. Before she could wrench away he had lifted and flung her twisting towards a chair in the corner of the room, which knocked over a pedestal and pot which smashed about her left shoulder. She heard him shouting as she crawled away: 'Thieving, lying bitch,' aware that he had snatched a hunting-crop from the mantelpiece and felt it now searing her back, neck and shoulders and she could hear herself screaming with terror and pain. She could not now make out what he was shouting, and when she got to the door she stumbled up limping and running away into the half-light till she reached the refuge of beech trees. She stood behind one and now heard his voice come hoarsely:

'Run, run, run, thief to thief, run to Ward, Rome's mug of Fenian poison; help him blow our world to bits ... I married a viper that hatched a viper ... Run, run, run, and keep running, you'll never get my fields, my gold!'

His voice suddenly sounded broken as he shouted again after a silence, 'Can you hear me, girl, run to the knife-grinder, out of this place and out of this life forever! Can you hear me? I never, ever want to see or hear you ever in my life again the longest day I live . . . can you hear me, girl . . . never.'

She had fallen to her knees scarcely able to breathe. When she heard the porch door and then the front door close, she got up, crossed the avenue and found a path down through the laurels into the middle of the scrubland. She kept going till she came to the trunk of an oak tree. There she sat leaning against it, holding her pulsing face with both hands. One eyebrow was cut and streaming blood. There was blood in her nose and in her mouth. Two of her bottom teeth felt loose. Her tongue felt thick and too big for her mouth. She still found it difficult to breathe.

Far away down to the left a startled blackbird called out. Then she heard what sounded like the crackle of dry twigs underfoot. Her breathing almost stopped completely, as she listened. Again a crackle further down and the sound of branches swishing together. Ward and Blessing? She stood, moved out a little into the open, aware that she could only see with one eye, the other was blurred. She covered it, staring down towards the county road and the bundle of odd-shaped fields that tumbled away in the half-light towards Brackagh and Ward's cottage in its thirty acres of whins and rocks. After a few minutes she saw them, two small dark figures emerging onto the county road. They stood talking for what seemed about ten minutes before parting, one heading down Clarna Brae towards Enniskillen, the other crossing the road and ditch and walking steadily towards the lower road. She had failed to keep her appointment with death. Clearly now they were looking for her, alive, to discover what had gone wrong.

There were clumps of reddish dock leaves growing in the area of light round the oak tree. She used some of them to clear the congealing blood from her lips and chin, aware now that the left side of her face was badly swollen, and that she could not close the fingers of her left hand. She continued to clean her face almost unaware of physical pain, her mind unable to take in what had happened and was still happening. And then she heard her voice saying, 'There's a grave somewhere here but no body to put in it.' Then she was saying: 'This is my body and this is my blood! What's God up to? All's wrong with the world!'

She began to make her way over and down through the laurels and rhododendron shrubbery towards the double ditch which led to the county road. She had played often in here as a child, knew exactly where the double ditch ran down the middle and the line that led to the dead ash tree drawn clearly on the Dummy's map. Ashes to dust. She could hear a thrush singing somewhere and paused to listen. How extraordinarily beautiful the world could be and all the creatures in it, excepting mankind.

To reach the ash tree she had to crawl through the undergrowth and there it was, exactly as described, a gash in the ground not quite six feet deep, a chilling rectangle with a pile of brown, yellow and bluish clay on one side mixed in with shards and stones and, standing against the tree, a spade she recognised – the handle a shaft cut out of the ditch with a black horn on top for leverage, a good Fermanagh spade she thought, just the job for burying old cows and dead girls. Lying at the base of the tree was a masonry hammer with a long steel-pointed edge on one side, and the rope, exactly as described. The Dummy was not imagining. She picked up the spade and looked at it and heard herself say:

'He loves me; he loves me not.'

She moved to the edge of the grave and stood looking down into it, remembering her mother's burial. This, a much nicer place to lie, she thought, I'd almost have picked it for myself, peace and quiet under the sun and moon, rain, wind and stars, what more could any girl want? She looked around the tree and up at the sky. Far below in the quarter-light, a scattering of small lakes in a haze of quilted fields and to her right, a necklace of green islands set in the lower lough and beyond them, fifty miles off, the bulk of Queen Maeve's tomb staring out to sea.

What words did they use across a table or in a public house? And what had they planned between them? How exactly would they do it? A rope round her neck, a savage blow to the skull, that spike to the brain, prostrate then and twitching with twisting mouth and eyes open like any dying beast tumbled into this hole to sleep forever with clay and stones and worms. And what if not dead? To waken even for a minute in that black, suffocating dark, Dear Christ, the terror! And again she could feel herself beginning to shake all over. Crying then so bitterly, so loudly, that a dog somewhere began to bark in response. When the emotion eased, she heard herself say distinctly:

'Dear God in heaven, will you punish him, my lover, Liam Ward? Answer me, God, because if not, let me tell you now that I will kill him, some way, somehow, somewhere, some day without pity and without guilt, or die trying; you have my oath on that.'

For a while she lay trying to think. Billy would

187

read her letter, learn what had happened, and regret his brutality. He would not howl as he did over her mother's grave but would feel wronged and more sorry for himself than for her. Going back to Clonoula was unthinkable. There could be no returning; that was the last place on earth. Where so? Where to now? Alive beside her grave in her best travelling clothes without a farthing, nothing but her grandmother's brooch and her mother's ring, which could not buy a railway ticket, food, or medical help. She could not borrow from any of Billy's wide acquaintances. Of two school friends, one was married in Southampton, the other in Fermoy. 'So where?' she said aloud. 'It's to Liam I go, to Liam Ward my love, that's my destiny for today, there's nowhere else to go.'

He would not be overjoyed to see her alive without gold. 'I have no choice . . . so be it.'

She got up, and crawled in the direction of the double ditch. When the scrub gave way to more open woodland, she began to walk until she found a path leading to the county road. She crossed it, going through the same gates and gaps that Ward had gone, continuing on towards Brackagh. The countryside was quiet, asleep; no sound but the crowing of cocks and the high whirring bleat of snipe. At McMahon's, and again at Rooney's, sheepdogs came barking from their front streets, across fences and across the fields she was crossing. Unafraid, she ignored them. Dogs were quick to recognise gender and seldom attacked females.

At the march of Rooney's land, she climbed through dead bracken onto the scutch-spined lane leading up towards Ward's cottage, from where she could look down to the small lake and watery bogs where she had helped him drag out a cow almost a year ago.

Darker then, returning with the key when he was burying the cow with Blinky Blessing. Undertakers. A pair. Heroes.

And of a sudden it seemed obvious to her that it must be natural for men to sit down together and plan the killing and burying of other men, women or children. She tried to imagine herself in the kitchen or the boiler-house at Clonoula talking with Mercy Boyle in such a way and the idea was so unthinkable, so ludicrous even to imagine that it must, she felt, be deeply unnatural. Now, for the first time, she became conscious of what was growing in her womb with a repulsion she would not have thought possible. She put the image forcibly from her mind and walked on up the lane.

The door of Ward's cottage was locked. She peered in the window, tried the back: also locked. Behind the water-barrel under the slated roof of a water-tank, she found the front-door key and let herself in. On the table there were two plates with rasher rinds smeared with egg. And two mugs and a half bottle of Jameson's Irish Whiskey. She stared at this for what seemed like a very long time: a murderers' meal. The hearth seemed dead and there was a feeling of bareness. The mantelpiece had been cleared. There were boxes under the long upright couch between the two small front windows, and alongside this couch a large trunk. She opened it and looked in. It was stuffed with shirts, trousers, jackets, socks and divided in two by rough boards. On the empty side there was one blanket. This was clearly the receptacle intended for Billy Winters' gold.

Innumerable times she had tried to imagine the bedroom off the kitchen, had visualised a white-washed room, a small, deep window, a brown clay-crazed floor, white-washed walls, a simple pine bed, a patchwork quilt, the smell of turf smoke. She opened the door and looked in. It was smaller than she had imagined, a personal smell competing with the smell of Lysol, the rumple of bedclothes on a very rough bed-frame, a cracked ewer, a smeared chamber pot. The white, bright walls she had imagined were yellow and as dirty-looking as the rumple of blankets. In the window a small mirror hung from a nail. In the greyish half-light, she looked into it to see Billy Winters' handiwork. Her left eye was completely closed, her left cheekbone grotesquely swollen. Two of her lower teeth wobbled. She put her forefinger on them and as she looked she realised as she often did that she was a mirror-image of her mother and how her mother would have looked from time to time long ago. She heard herself say, 'May God forgive you, Billy Winters, because I won't.'

Back in the kitchen she looked through the drawers of the dresser till she found a knife that seemed right. She placed it under a pillow in the bedroom, stood looking at the pillow and thinking about this realised it would be discovered or wrenched from her hand. She returned it to the drawer. Whatever opportunity arose she would have to be certain of the outcome. She was aware that she was cold. Indifferent to it she sat at the kitchen table leafing through pages of *The Farmer's Journal and Impartial Reporter*. There were unconfirmed rumours that Lord Erne's American bride had arrived with a dowry of twelve million dollars. Mr Percy French of world renown, etc. A bullock at Clones had attacked the Celtic Cross and had been put down by firearms from the local barracks. Mr Shirley of Carrickmacross would be giving an historical lecture on his 'History of Monaghan' at the end of the month in the Town Hall. Sir John Lentaigne, Inspector of Schools, would be a member of the fishing-party staying with Lord Rossmore. She then read in full about the hunger at Glencolumbkille and went on then to read advertisements:

To Canada
For three pounds.
Holloway's Pills; for purity of blood.
Important discovery!
No more suffering!
Painless dentistry.

Then to general news and headings:

ARRESTS IN LONDON AND BIRMINGHAM.
SEIZURE OF ENORMOUS QUANTITIES
OF NITRO-GLYCERINE.
EXECUTION OF JOE BRADY LAST AND YOUNGEST
OF THE PHOENIX PARK MURDERERS.
DAY APPOINTED, THURSDAY MAY 17th 1883.
THE PHILADELPHIA PARTY AND MR PARNELL.

On Monday morning a man residing within a mile of Maguire's Bridge cut his daughter's throat and afterwards his own. The coroner said both appeared famished in the extreme.

At the bottom of the page there was an advertisement which said:

HOW THE POOR LIVE
by George R. Sims

She turned to another page.

In the column alongside this she read that: '*John Gillis, auctioneer and valuer, was selling unreservedly the lease of a farm of land at Brackagh, six miles from Enniskillen, well watered and fenced, also a draycart and two strong working horses. Held as a yearly tenancy under William Hudson Winters at the judicial rent of twelve pounds per annum.*' She stopped reading and stared at the two blue-banded mugs, stained inside, at the plates smeared with egg and stringy chewed lumps of rasher rinds, the empty bottle of whiskey and the two glasses that looked cloudy even in candlelight. With hand and forearm, she pushed them all over the edge of the table. They clattered down, breaking and splintering as she rested her head in the crook of her arm, on the side of her face that was not throbbing. She blew out the candle, indifferent to the cold. It was only after a few minutes when she felt the cooling wetness on her arms that she realised she was crying.

13

Where was she now? Had she lost her nerve? Changed her mind? Gone off with Billy's gold alone? No. He would have to persuade her to try again next week. Unless for some reason she had used the farmpass to the low road that bypassed the main avenue? Blinky had caught McCafferty's mare and gone galloping to Enniskillen to watch if she boarded the early goods train for Belfast. He himself had climbed to Carn above the marble arches to see what he could see moving on either high or low road. Nothing. It was cold. In the sky there was a glow, a hint of the coming day. The moon had gone. Far below the crows were raucous in the beech trees around Clonoula. He went back down carefully avoiding farmyards, unable to avoid thinking of the business on hand.

When he reached the long bog near Blessing's cottage, he sat on a turf clamp, rolled a cigarette, lit it and sat waiting, watching, listening for Blinky's return. One blow. Death would come so quick she would scarce know she had died, a shot pigeon or squirrel tumbling to earth. Useless to pretend that her eyes would not be staring at him through sleep; that her voice would not sound in other women's voices, the warmth of her body in other women's, and all the while he would know she was buried deep at Clonoula. The rawest whiskey in strange places and far cities could not bury it from memory and dreams. All this he half-knew. Also he knew absolutely what the note brought by young Courtney meant. It read:

'Ward: give back what you've stolen or be got yourself. Be certain of this before May ends.'

A blunt warning. Blunt justice would follow as surely as it followed his uncle-in-law, James Carey, killed a few days ago at Port Elizabeth. They would follow and get him on a double count. He was a connection of James Carey's, the most hated man in Ireland, and he had 'stolen' their funds; in his own mind, he had borrowed. They were calling it theft. To attempt Billy Winters' gold any other way would be dangerous; let her steal it, then steal from her. The present plan was undetectable and had come about almost accidentally. Talking politics with Blinky one night, both drunk in his cottage, they had talked of guns from Germany shipped here to finish the job Parnell had 'not the guts to finish'. Then almost unthinkingly he had said:

'If I could make her get Billy's gold, then bury her, we'd have guns and stuff enough to blow them all to hell out of here.'

'Bury,' Blinky had repeated.

'Yes,' he had said, 'bury'. Blinky had gone into a reverie, his mouth slightly open. When he came out of it he suddenly banged his fist on the table:

'Christ, man, but that's the smartest move I ever heard tell of, they'd be hunting her the world over and she'd never be got 'cause she couldn't be got . . . not six feet under.'

The next day with sobriety he was less certain. Afraid of seeming afraid he had blustered approval. From then on the plan had grown to where and when and how. Thus far it was not going as they had planned.

From a long way off, he heard the sound of steel-shod hooves on the dark road, then silence. Five minutes later he saw a figure at the other end of the bog. It could only be Blinky making his way homewards. Ward stood; Blinky saw him and began walking towards him:

'Well?'

'Nothin' . . . you?'

'Nothing.'

'Jesus, where is she, Liam?'

'Still above, asleep maybe.'

'Maybe she got afeard and changed her mind or maybe somethin's wrong . . . maybe Billy catched her at the safe.'

'Doped and footless?' Ward shook his head.

'He'd straighten and sharpen if he thought his gold was for the high sea . . . Christ I'm hungry, are you?'

'You're always hungry, Blinky.'

They began to walk, threading their way through lines of drying turf towards the thatched roof of Blessing's cabin in a hollow, a wisp of smoke twisting from the single chimney.

'Someone's on the move early,' Ward said.

'That's Mammywee – she be's up footerin' half the night then sleepin' half the day; contrariness!'

As they went down a stone lane leading to the back of the cottage they heard a high-pitched call that sounded like: 'Heyaw . . . hengs! Hengs! Hengs! Hengs! Heway!' and then the rattle of a bucket and the noise of ducks, geese and hens flapping, and bantams flying out of the low ash trees behind the cabin.

'That's what the brother calls "the Chinese hen call",' Blinky said.

When Mary Blessing saw that her son was talking to someone through the side of his mouth she moved from near the doorway out into the middle of the street and called out:

'That you Attie? what bould scrap is traipsin' the country with you at this hour? Have yous no shame?'

'It's no scrap, Mammywee.'

'Someone's jookin' behind the gable: I seen her.'

'*Him*: it's our friend and neighbour, Liam Ward.'

'Surely to God he's not hidin' from me . . . is he?'

Ward stepped out from the gable to where he could see Mary Blessing, a tall dumb-bell-shaped woman with brown unblinking eyes set in a halo of white hair; as good-looking a woman as her son Blinky was ugly:

'Not hiding Mam,' Ward said, 'I'm on my way home.'

'And well you should be, son: what has the pair of you out till this ungodly hour?'

Neither Ward nor Blinky replied. Mary Blessing persisted:

'Is it God's work? or the devil's?'

'Neither,' Blinky said.

'Whose so?'

'Ireland's,' Blinky said.

Mary Blessing changed her bucket of mash from the right hand to the left, blessed herself and said:

'Is it patriots yous are . . . Fenians?'

When neither Ward nor Blinky responded, she said:

'If yous are caught stealing that stuff from Billy Winters' quarry they'll lock you away forever.'

'We'll not be caught at anything,' Blinky said.

During this exchange Ward's expression did not alter. After a silence Mary Blessing said:

'Come in so, yous are bound to be hungry.'

When Ward shook his head and made to move away, Mary Blessing's voice went up a register:

'You're not away to an empy house, Liam, and you up all night . . . you'll come in for five minutes and ate what's ready here.'

Blinky now muttered to Ward:

'You'd best not offend Mammywee.'

Ward shrugged almost inperceptibly and followed mother and son into the warm firelit kitchen. They sat at the table facing the hearth as Mary Blessing dropped the kettle two notches and swung the crook over the flame, ladling porridge from a pot on the hearth into two bowls. She then set about putting milk, scones and butter on the table, lit a candle, turning up the wick of the paraffin lamp which hung between an oleograph of Saint Patrick banishing the snakes from Ireland and a picture of Pope Pius the Ninth smiling infallibly and blessing the Blessing kitchen in Fermanagh. Mary poured herself a mug of tea and sat on a creepie in the hearth opposite Ward. She was looking directly into his eyes as she said:

'I've only the two sons left out of the dozen I reared. The poet fella inside never laves the bed and this fella here's hardly ever in it!'

Ward smiled remotely as she went on.

'Itself did yous have any success at all last night?' Blinky began to blink rapidly, stopped eating and craned round to look in Ward's face, got no help and said:

'That story has to travel on a bit yet.'

'Liam, you're a man of the world and they say a

clever man, can you keep this cratur of mine out of harm's way?'

It was a direct question. Ward was forced to reply:

'He's wit enough and fit enough to mind himself.'

'Like too many in this country all wit and no sense.'

The bedroom door alongside the hearth opened and Wishie Blessing appeared, barefoot, yawning, a railway greatcoat over his nightshirt. He was peering through bottle-end spectacles, a week's stubble on his face. Mary Blessing greeted her son as he padded towards the front door:

'You'll take a bowl of stirabout, Wishie son?'

'Naw.'

'A mug of tay?'

'Naw.'

'A griddle scone?'

'Naw.'

'You want nothin'?'

'Naw.'

'No breakfast at all?'

'Naw.'

Wishie was now out of sight. As the splash of urine came hissing noisily off the cutstone gully near the front door, Blinky leaned over to Ward and whispered:

'The bard of Brackagh adds his bladderful!'

Ward was still smiling as Wishie came back to the kitchen. He paused looking at the food on the table, then glanced up at the clock on the mantel-shelf. Again Mary Blessing pressed him to eat something. This time he responded sharply:

'It's the middle of the friggin' night . . . who could ate breakfast? Where were these two hoeboys till this hour?'

'On Ireland's business,' Mary Blessing said.

'That a fact!'

'That's what they tell me.'

'Manoeuvres is it lads?' Wishie asked. 'Are yous plannin' to take over Dublin Castle next weekend?'

'Bates lying up in bed,' Blinky said, 'writin' ballads and playing with your mickey.'

Wishie did not respond to this jibe except to mutter as he left the kitchen:

'Crude bollocks.'

Mary Blessing got up, lifted the teapot and said:

'Yous'll break the weather with that bad talk; and *you* Attie, you shouldn't annoy him like that ... he can't help himself in the morning, poor Wishie, and the father was identical: very slow to wake. And if he does seem a bit sour of himself I can tell you he writes the sweetest wee poems ever you seen, about the wee twisty roads and the wee humpy fields and the windy rivers and the holy wells and the great loughs. And the best ones of all are about the black-hearted villains who stole our land and murdered and starved us these hundreds of years, and how hell's not torture enough for what they done to us.'

'It'll take more than one of Wishie's ballads to shift the like of Billy Winters or Lord Erne.'

'Jape all yous want ... our Wishie's a different breed of patriot, that's all; and every bit as good as either of ye.'

Ward stood suddenly and began moving towards the door saying:

'That was a good breakfast, thank you, Mam.'

'Sure you ate less than a wee banty ... are you craw-sick, son?'

'Craw-full, Mam.'

Blinky followed him out and walked with him as far

as the gable of the house. When well out of earshot, Blinky said:

'If you hear tell of anythin' get word to me.'

'About what?' Ward asked, 'there's nothin' to tell. We'll bide our time and try again.'

Blinky watched Ward walk away into a shoulder-high mist which had risen and thickened, spreading all over Brackagh bog in the coming light.

He then left the apron of stoned ground at the gable, went down the rutted lane, overgrown on either side with knotted ash and blackthorn, until he came to an iron gate. He climbed it, found an area in the double ditch, stooped, relieved himself and stayed hunkered facing out towards the mist unfolding over the haggard meadow.

As he grasped a handful of dry dead bracken fronds he half-stood suddenly, startled, blinking rapidly, listening, one hand hoisting his trousers, the other bunching the bracken in sudden fright. He could not make sense of the sounds nor put on them a familiar image. At first they seemed like a sow rooting and grunting through clods of earth, then it changed to a high pitched singing and humming which seemed human, followed by guttural sounds like foreign words. Some madman escaped from Monaghan asylum? Some neighbour who'd lost his wits? or worse, the Garvarry ghost, which his mother said went all round Ulster with a turf barrow gathering up the dead.

Both saw each other at the same instant: the Dummy McGonnell with his lips drawn back aggressively, his nose twitching grotesquely in response to Blinky's function. Blinky's staring eyes were now fibrillating with relief.

'Ah, yah wandery auld cunt; you put the heart across me!'

The Dummy drew back his lips like a horse that's bitten a sour apple. He then put his thumb and forefinger to block his nostrils, turned sideways to let Blinky see his gesture in outline, glancing back every now and then grinning, lip-reading Blinky's further abuse.

When almost out of sight in the mist he stopped and turned back to Blinky who now had thumbed up his braces and stepped out of the ditch. There was about fifty yards between them. As Blinky was about to utter more invective the Dummy began what seemed like a dance, lifting his right foot high, his two arms curved over it and then all three moving together in unison as Blinky shouted:

'You mad frigger! What the hell are you at? go back and dance some other place; do you think you're a fucken railway engine?'

The Dummy suddenly stopped, shook his head and repeated the mime, slowly finishing it with an uplift of both hands, a gesture of throwing clay over his shoulder. He kept up this digging mime as Blinky watched, his mouth open, transfixed. The Dummy stopped and grinned again. He could see fear, puzzlement and disbelief in Blinky's face as he asked in a subdued, almost frightened voice:

'Are you after a job cutting turf? Is that it?' The Dummy shook his head slowly, smiling, and stared at the ground making low grunting noises of contempt. Suddenly and it seemed almost violently he pointed straight at Blinky and the grunting became a kind of hysterical high-pitched accusing sound.

'What in the hell is wrong with you now!' Blinky shouted.

The Dummy could see that Blinky's face had gone very white, a kind of blinking death mask. With a gesture of obscene comtempt, he turned and walked away down the haggard field out of sight. Long after he was gone, Blinky could hear the odd gurgling sounds and a kind of mad laughing. Only when the sounds had gone completely did he realise that he was still holding the handful of bracken. It was trembling in his hand.

14

From a long way off she could sense Ward's approach.
It was nothing she could hear. She went to the front
window of the cottage; nothing to see but the street and
Laban Lake set in its landscape of bare tussocked fields
on either side giving way to spongy bogland of heather,
bracken, rock and rough grasses. As she was about to
turn away from the small window, a dark figure came
up from the hollow of the lane. It could only be him,
Ward, nobody else. Aloud, she heard herself say:

'In the dove-grey light he comes, my love Liam, my
hero comes.'

Her heart began to hobble painfully. She wanted to
turn away, to cry! She forced herself to keep watching.
With a great intake of breath her heart steadied and her
vision cleared. Yes, there he was, still coming well up
into the landscape now, walking steadily up the rutted
lane leading from the lake towards the cottage. He would
be about five minutes. Where to be? How to be? She
had been awake all night into the dawn, brutally beaten,
shown the road by Billy Winters. It would be normal
enough for her now to lie either on a couch or across
the table and pretend to be sleeping.

She got a rug and pillow from the bedroom, put the rug round her shoulders, the pillow on the table, closed her eyes and turned her swollen face so that he would see the bruised congested cheek, the closed eye, her swollen hand resting alongside her head, now grossly welted and enlarged where it had been struck by the hunting-crop. He would stare for a while, then waken her. She tried to imagine his face, his eyes, his first words. These imaginings so agitated her that again she found it difficult to breathe. She heard the footsteps approach and stop. He would be looking at the key in the door, trying to make out who was inside, guessing that perhaps it was her. She became aware of cold dawn air as the door opened. She knew Ward was standing now in the kitchen looking at her, trying to make sense of what he was seeing. Then his hand on her shoulder. She waited a few moments, opened her eyes which immediately found his:

'Jesus Christ,' he muttered, 'he got you taking it?'

She was looking up into his face trying to discover what she must have missed before. Nothing different. The same face, the same slightly odd squint, same irregular teeth. It was not the face of a murderer. He was less than three feet away and looking at her very closely:

'Yes, he caught me.'

'Didn't you give him the bromides?'

'He spilled some whiskey, maybe he got sick, anyway they didn't work. I was at the safe. He got me with my hands in his treasure; didn't you hear him shouting like a bull?'

'W . . . I heard nothing.'

He had almost said 'we'. This so electrified her that she almost said 'you and who?'

'What was he shouting?'

'I'll give you death and nightingales . . . you'll fly from here, forever, with rooks, daws and magpies, you'll croak like scald crows from now on with fellow thieves and vermin. Things like that.'

She was watching his face. He was not as she had imagined he would be; he was in no way evasive. If anything he seemed angry. She had bungled, been caught. He and Blinky had not managed to bury her and get away with the gold. It had gone wrong, it was her fault. She found herself more fascinated by what he must be thinking than what she herself was feeling, like a nightmare until she realised she was laughing oddly, almost hysterically. Through this she heard Ward say:

'It's not funny . . . we're bogged now.'

'We have our two selves,' she said. 'We're young, we have our health, we're not being hunted by Constabulary, we don't have to hide, we can walk out of this house and sail away to a new life, to another world . . . maybe it's our good fortune.'

'We've no fortune, we've nothing.'

'You'll get something for the lease of this place. Eighty, a hundred pounds: that's ten times more than a million others who left here. Anyway, they say people with a lot of money are seldom happy, they say "show me a rich man and I'll show you a brute," and I say Billy Winters isn't a happy man and he has a lot of money. He's never happy except when he's drunk and then he's hateful, but you know all that . . . you're now my white knight, Liam, my hero, my saviour, my lover, my husband-to-be, the father of our children-to-be . . . my protector, my defender, my guardian angel, can you not forgive me, love, for bungling?'

'There's nothin' to forgive.'

She could sense him looking at her with a curious

expression, almost now she thought with more hatred than anger. Could hatred be infectious? Maybe he now felt what she was feeling, or could he sense the mockery aimed in her every word.

'This is the first day proper of our new life, May 4th, our elopement day; a bit unlucky maybe, but they say a bad start bodes a good finish. I wasn't happy at the idea of stealing because I've never stolen as much as a farthing in my whole life so far from anyone, but for you, my love, I was willing to rob my guardian, take every ounce of gold he had. She paused, waiting for him to respond. He kept looking at her with an expression she now found repulsive. It made her say:

'You took no risk, you paid no penalty, lost nothing; I've lost everything and maybe now without the gold you don't want me, don't love me.'

'That's not true,' Ward said in a flat voice.

'You can prove that now, you could murder Billy Winters, take his gold; we could leave then together as planned.'

She could see his eyes dilating as he thought about this. She had not meant the idea to be considered, thought he would dismiss it out of hand.

'Today would be a bad day to try that out.'

'Well then, tomorrow, next week, next month? He deserves to die. Do you think you could do it, love?'

Again she could see that Ward was looking at her intently and now said:

'You're talking very odd.'

'Am I?'

'Very.'

Outside there was a frenetic hissing followed by heavy wingbeats, then a hoarse voice whispering urgently:

'Go way, go to hell, quit, will yous go way, go way.'

Ward crossed to the small window and peered out as Beth asked:

'A visitor? At dawn!'

'It's nobody,' Ward muttered as he moved towards the door.

'Does "nobody" have a name,' she asked.

He glanced back at her, muttering as he went out to the street:

'Blinky Blessing . . . Drunk most likely.'

He could tell at once that Blinky was unnerved. He met this nervousness with a cold stare and a faint head-jerk to indicate someone in the cottage. Alerted, Blinky looked from door to window making a silent round with his mouth which asked 'Who?' Ward answered in something less than a whisper:

'The Winters girl. Billy waked; kicked her out.'

'What's she doin' here?'

'She's no place else to go.'

Blinky took Ward's arm and led him away from the cottage talking very quietly as he went:

'I'll tell you why I'm here, Liam.'

'You shouldn't be.'

'Hold on! I was hunkered below in the ditch after you left when the Dummy McGonnell come by in our front meadow. We saw each other at the one time.'

Blinky swallowed, his eyes dilating.

'Go on, go on.'

'I think he knows somethin', Liam.'

'What could he know? He's deaf and dumb!'

'Not blind . . . and he's a cute auld hoor.'

'Go on.'

Blinky glanced back at the cottage door and ran his tongue along his top lip.

'After he seen me in the ditch he begun to make all

kinds of faces and ciphers, you know the way he carries on, so I shouted at him.' Blinky imitated the Dummy's digging motion, then looked directly into Ward's face.

'It give me the quare scare.' Ward's expression did not change, his eyes dropped from Blinky's ravaged face to the street.

'What do you think, Liam?'

Ward looked away up to Carn. They could hear two cocks and a jackass welcoming the growing light. Blinky kept studying Ward's face:

'Suppose he goes to the Constabulary?'

'About what . . . there's no law agin digging a hole in the ground.'

'Aye, true, that's all we done.'

'Anyway, he meant you should have brought a spade to bury your shit.'

'You think?'

'Most likely.'

'Christ, you could be right, Liam.'

'You're a nervy bloody man; she's going to wonder now what in hell you're doing here.'

'Maybe it's all for luck.'

Ward looked away coldly.

'Is this your notion of luck?'

'Well if Billy hadn't catched her the way he did, she'd've catched her death from us, and if the Dummy seen us, we'd've catched our death at the end of a rope; an unlucky night's work.'

'You're still drunk.'

'I could never have faced it sober. Even if it went right a while back, it might have stayed wrong ever after and a body can't stay drunk forever.'

'The whole thing,' Ward said, 'is a bungle; we've missed a king's ransom and I'm bogged with this one.'

Blinky began to giggle and then winked.

'Be God, Liam,' he said, 'she's laid on handy now, like a pump in the yard; let her bake and scrub, make use of her, throw the leg across at night!'

Ward studied Blinky's face:

'You're an eejit, Blinky.'

'Am I? What does that make you but an eejit's comrade?'

Blinky grinned and added:

'There's a pair of us in it, Liam, and I'll tell you for more . . .'

His expression suddenly changed:

'Your one inside is at the door this minute lookin' at the two of us.'

Ward turned and said matter-of-factly:

'Blinky here's on the tear, wants to borrow a mouthful of whiskey.'

Ward walked away from Blinky towards the cottage door. Beth went inside, and Ward entered followed by Blinky saluting clownishly with his right forefinger at his right eyebrow. He was licking his lips. Beth could see that his mouth was dry, his eyes blinking, inflamed. The Dummy's caricature was accurate. She could also see at a glance the putty-coloured clay on his boots; the clay of her grave. Murder boots. No clay on Ward's boots. Too fastidious? Too lazy to dig? 'You're getting a heap of gold for a small labour Blinky, all you have to do is kill her quick and bury her deep.'

It was all too incredible to take in. Now here they were, both standing in front of her. As she looked from one to the other, she wondered how they had planned it. How would she have been enticed from the avenue into the scrub? Ward would have stopped her. Some pretext. A whispered word. Some change of plan, my love. Some problem about a train time. As he talked Blinky, from behind the tree or a rhododendron would act: that blunt hammer with the spike. Or with a club: a single blow to the skull. The spike doubtful. Too much blood. Garrotting? What was that? A rope tightened round the neck. Unable to scream, staring into her lover's eyes. Blinky choking her from behind?

She felt her heart slow again as the images recurred, aware that blood was draining from her face. Seeing them side by side, she imagined what it would be like if *they* were roped back to back on the floor. How easy, how simple it would be to cut their throats one by one, Blinky first, then Ward. Kiss first, then kill. Vengeance, truly horrible, the blood spraying her skirt. That, she thought, would be more distasteful than slitting their gullets. It calmed her to think of this. The violence of feeling and images was so strong that she looked away lest they could read in her face the repulsion she felt.

Ward had opened the cupboard of the dresser, took out a half-bottle of whiskey, placed it on a shelf of the dresser as Blinky crossed to the corner and lifted out a porringer of water from a cask. He drank greedily, refilling the porringer and then tipping it into a glass which he held up saying:

'The best water in Ulster, Miss; see . . . blue; pure, a woman body in this house'd be off to a good start with water like that.'

She could see him looking closely at her face as his eyes became accustomed to the poor interior light.

'Liam was just tellin' me you got a hammerin' above . . . You wouldn't be the first woman whipped by that fella. You're well away from that house – and you neither kith nor kin.'

She stared at him without replying, watching him drink

the second pint of water, his adam's apple pulsating. He put the glass down, pulled a black-nailed claw across his forehead removing the hair from his eyes. He then stood holding his cap in front of his testicles.

'That would make me a bastard,' she said.

Blinky exploded with laughter and elbowed Ward:

'Better that than any blood of Billy Winters'; the grandfather and his grandfather before him was a terror to the world, the worst breed of landlord, highwayman more or less ... robbers of the Irish people ... am I right, Liam?'

'High seas man,' Ward corrected.

'A what?' Blinky asked.

'He was a class of pirate, the first of the Winters.'

All the time she could see Blinky was watching her face very closely. Now he said:

'Boysadear, Miss, but you got a woeful hammerin'; thon face of yours is a fright!'

'More a birthday treat,' Beth said.

She tapped at her swollen face, smiled back, and said:

'Fist and horse-whip.'

Ward and Blinky glanced at each other. Neither spoke. Beth went on:

'He must have heard from someone, Liam, that we were "great" and you being a tenant, *that* in Billy's book means a gale-day liar, a debtor, a latter-day Fermanagh bush-kerne, a witless spade-man, a hired spalpeen, a stable brat, the lowest of the low, a landless Paddy, a less-than-nothing nobody, and, being unavailable for punishment, he took the whip to me! It's common enough the world over.'

She touched her face again and said:

'Must be millions like me, whipped half-blind by

blind-drunk men, for this, that and the other . . . or nothing.'

'Song,' Blinky said, 'he didn't spike the run of your tongue, Miss.'

'No, and you're a wit of sorts yourself I'm told.'

Blinky grinned yellow teeth at her:

'Who says that?'

'Mercy Boyle tells me you're a witty man, full of "spakes" she says.'

'Mercy, is it?'

'Mercy Boyle . . . She swears it's the goats' milk you and Wishie take to bed every night in a baby's bottle.'

Blinky's grinning teeth vanished suddenly.

'She's a liar then,' he hissed.

'I couldn't believe it either. Not Attie, I said; maybe the brother Wishie, the bard, but Attie's much too manly, I said . . . he's a butcher.'

Blinky stared at her uncertain, lifted the half-full bottle of whiskey and said through the side of his mouth:

'That's the only bottle I bother with night or day.'

He moved towards the door, turned awkwardly:

'Good luck to you now, Miss Winters, you'll need all the luck that's goin'.'

'May God go with you, Attie Blessing, *and* his blessed mother *and* may all the angels and saints guard and defend you.'

Blinky's mouth opened a bit. He stared with disbelief, glanced at Ward, shrugged, then suddenly left.

15

As Ward moved to close the door, Beth knelt by the hearth where she began raking through the ashes. She knew that Ward was standing behind her, could feel his eyes:

'Have you matches, Liam?'

'On the salt box.'

She placed a bruss of heather and broken twigs on top of crumpled newspaper, lit the paper. Pulling the crook over she lowered the kettle two notches down onto the flames:

'My grandmother, my mother's mother over in Tirkennedy had a fire like this in a house like this. The boast was it never went out for a hundred years. A shroud-maker she was during the famine; only for the trade in death-robes, they'd all have died of hunger. They all clung to the pot when there was nothing to put in it but they were all buried decent. Terrible times. It's left us all half-hungry and mad greedy, or that's what they say. Only for all those shrouds, I wouldn't be here now wondering how you're going to kill Billy Winters.' She didn't look round. There was quite a silence before Ward said, 'Quit the talk of killing will you; there's going to be no killing.'

'No?'

'No.'

'You're right . . . This is our honeymoon in the magic month. We're eloping, Liam; this is our love-cabin and all the world is warming, the brown in the mountains is greening, Christ is risen and we're alone now that your friend Blinky is gone.'

'He's no friend.'

'But you work through him and with him. He helped you bury that cow a year ago the day we met; he helps you cut turf, he helps you in the quarry, helps you make your hay: he's your friend, Liam.'

'He's a neighbour; I pay him. He's no friend.'

'I'm glad. It's the screechy noise he makes through the side of his mouth and the bony look of him . . . though Mary Blessing must be proud of him, she's like a dumb-bell herself, a big proud dumb belle . . . Can you imagine sitting in that house, listening to the two of them squawking at each other? I'd rather spend a night in hell . . . I'm glad he's not your friend, Liam, but in truth, love, he is a friend *of sorts*, is he not?'

She turned round. Ward was looking at her, his expression impassive; then he said quietly:

'It doesn't matter what he is.'

'Oh but it does, if he was your brother you couldn't help that – not your fault; but *friends* you *pick*, and they do matter, but in a way you're right. We'll be on the high seas soon, or have you other plans now? You see I've been thinking and thinking and thinking. This place could be lovely but it needs a woman's hand; there's a smell in your bedroom, love: stale, we can freshen it. Out of the back window you can see a hazel hedge and bracken, you can cook and eat the little fronds of bracken and there's wild rosemary and foxglove and bog-thyme and wild garlic and acres and acres of meadowsweet; we could stuff our pillows with that and sleep for centuries. And then there's no end of bilberries for jelly and wine and you've got ash and whitethorn: you can make chutney from ash keys and haws; and I know you have rhubarb and we could grow potatoes, and you could put in a stripe of barley. Even without a cow this little place could be a kind of paradise and you could catch fish with that otter-board miraculously, but a man can't live on fish and barley only. You could run "the cratur" for yourself. I wouldn't be jealous: it wouldn't blight our bed would it? You're too long-headed Liam, too far-thinking to get drunk every night. But I'm wondering why we must run away from paradise? If you pay rent to Billy Winters, you can stay here; we'd be the happiest people in the world. I'd make damson wine and we could eat trout with new potatoes. I'd go to the bog with you, you could cut and I could catch, and maybe in time we'd have children who could wheel and spread and turn.'

She missed a mutter from Ward and said:

'I didn't hear that.'

'You're raving, I said.'

'I'm sorry, love, he knocked my wits sideways, I'll try to talk less but talk I must, true love they say never runs smooth and if all the maxims come true finally, then you must believe that true love conquers all, in the end!'

'You're still raving.'

'Then I'll stay quiet and listen. Tell me, what are we to do?'

'You can't stay here.'

'I know that.'

'And *I* can't leave yet.'

'But we were both leaving this morning!'

'That was different . . . you can't stay here now.'

'Why?'

'Because every beggar goin' the road, every other huntsman, every school child, every nosy old woman for twenty townlands would know you were here . . . there'd be talk. Billy Winters'd come, then you know what'd happen.'

'Tell me what would happen?'

'He'd take the whip to you again, maybe, and to me if I let him.'

'Are you afraid of Billy Winters?'

'Afraid for you.'

'Then tell me what you plan, what's in your mind, love?'

'You'll have to go.'

'Where can I go? tell me where can I go? I've nowhere to go!'

'You must have friends.'

'I can't live with friends; I want to be with you. Why can't I stay? Nobody need know. I'll stay inside; I can use that pot in your bedroom and you could empty it for me. I'd do the same for you if you were sick or hiding. For you, for love I stole, what can you do for me? You took no risk, you've not been whipped or driven out, you've lost nothing, love, and if young girls can strangle infants, surely you can dispatch a hateful, brutal man for me, for love.'

She paused and added quietly:

'And for gold?'

'You said you loved Billy Winters in a way.'

'No longer, I now have murder in my heart.'

'It's stupid; I'd be caught and hung.'

'But death is a little thing, so everyone says.' Ward shrugged angrily and moved away.

'I thought you might jump on him, the way you

216

jumped on that rat, remember; but if you can't, you can't. Anyway it's better to rue going than to wait around forever, there's a tide in the affairs of men, a moon in the affairs of women and they say a bad start bodes a good finish. Why don't you answer, love?'

'About what?'

'Where I must go.'

'Elsewhere, and you'll have to stop talking . . . you're making my head light.'

In the silence that followed, she watched as he stood at the open half-door looking out into the street, his face angled away. There was no way of telling what was in that mind. Anger? Guilt? Boredom? A mix of all three. So great was her curiosity, she was tempted to say now, 'I saw where you were digging my grave with Blinky Blessing so I expect this conversation must be very odd for you, certainly it's very odd for me.' What would he do? Give one startled glance, walk out of the house like his father, and away forever? Small punishment for the most callous and mortal of crimes. Aloud she asked:

'Where elsewhere?'

Ward glanced round:

'You wait for me in London or Boston, when I've this place off my hands I'll follow.'

He could lie so easily, so effortlessly. He wanted her gone from his house; away elsewhere, anywhere. She was a nuisance now, useless. Again she felt hatred deepen and an almost deeper anger with herself for being so stupid:

'No matter where I am or where you are,' she said, 'we'll have to pick a name. It's going to be Christmas, love, or thereabouts; that'll narrow the choice depending on gender.' Ward did not react or seem to so she went on: 'Nicholas if it's a boy, how about Nicholas? I don't think you're listening fully, love . . . I'd no idea I'd find myself thinking so much about names but Nicholas I think is quite good. You expect Nicholas Ward to be somebody and of course he would be because he'd be your son, Liam, and mine. And then again if it's not a boy, which is of course what a girl is, we'd have to settle for Noelle, Nicola, Noleen, all of them somehow shrill; you feel they bite their nails and tend to be nervy, prone to fainting fits, silly a bit, given to talking overmuch like me: when I'm upset.'

He had turned and was walking towards her. She kept talking:

'Corrie, that's a good name, the Corry's are a branch of the Maguire clan, a good Fermanagh name; Corrie Ward: now she sounds clever, wide awake. You feel she could give a good account of herself, manage her life, because none of us can tell what we'll stumble into in the next ditch. Last week on a lovely April morning, there was a dead rat in the hall . . . a long-tailed brute: Terrible.'

She was unprepared for the effect, imagining he would shrug it off or feign a smile. His face not only looked suddenly haggard but the unreadable eyes seemed suddenly vulnerable:

'You shouldn't've kept that from me till now.'

'What better day? It's my birthday, the first day of our new life together, so I thought I'll tell you as we leave together.'

Astonishingly, incredibly, he was now hunkered beside her, his arms around her so that her chin was resting on his shoulder. She could see his neck, the dark hair curling at the nape, the whiteness of his skin, the familiar smell of whiskey and tobacco, and what she felt now was an extraordinary feeling of both revulsion and pity; like that March day long ago when a farmer called Irwin had tracked their sheepdog from the Cuilcagh Mountains to the back yard at Clonoula. The dog had come in trailing one shattered leg. She could remember the angry look of the farmer and his voice saying to Jim Ruttledge:

'There was a yella dog with this brute, I got *him*; he's dead . . . Between them they've kilt six ewes and eleven lambs.'

When Jim Ruttledge had gone in with the farmer to talk with Billy she remembered how she had looked and looked into the dog's gentle eyes, trying to understand the savagery that had driven it to kill and kill and kill. When Jim Ruttledge came back out, he said what any country man would say:

'Only one thing you can do with a bad dog, put him down; no choice.'

Now on Ward's shoulder she said quietly:

'Yes, I'll have to do that, I've no choice.'

Ward kept his arm round her. She could feel a slight trembling. She drew back. Pulling his face round she was astonished to see his eyes were glazed over with tears:

'Crying, love? Really and truly crying . . . are you?'

For a moment Ward was unable to answer. When composure returned he said:

'I'd no notion you were that way.'

'Nature's a terrible tinker, full of tricks and contrariness.'

True, because that moment of emotion just now, as he hunkered close, was real. All right to butcher her for Billy's gold, not all right to bury his own child within her. That was upsetting. Poor fellow, all of a-tremble, almost in tears. Clearly a heart of gold. It would have to be wrenched out of him and left for rats, scaldcrows.

'I know where I can go,' she said, 'Corvey Island.' Ward looked at her. She could see that he was relieved at the idea of her going anywhere. He muttered, 'You'll have to eat . . . you'd starve out there.'

'It's only for a few days, a week at most till you're finished here. I can live on bread, butter, watercress, black tea . . . that's no hardship.'

'You could be right,' he said.

'I know I am.'

Without looking at her or making further comment, he went to the dresser and began to gather bread, butter, tea and sugar. She watched him fold the tea and sugar into small squares of brown paper, wrap the bread in a sheet of newspaper. She then saw that he was putting butter into a dish, covering it with a saucer:

'I don't need the bowl and saucer.'

'The paper print,' Ward said, 'it'll stain the butter . . . blacken it.'

She looked at the back of his head with disbelief. The words 'stain' and 'blacken' echoing darkly in her mind. She could be lying now in the blackness of a grave, blood-stained, and here he was talking about ink stains on butter. He put the butter in a bowl, covered it with a saucer, wrapped both in newspaper and put all into a small hessian bag. He then turned to look at her, clearly relieved that she was leaving:

'We should go; it'll be broad daylight in an hour.'

She got up from the hearth, walked towards the door and out onto the street, watching as he locked the door of his cottage. Conscious of the grey stillness, the calm beauty of the bog, she heard herself say:

'Farewell, paradise . . .'

Ward did not respond. As he put the key in his pocket she asked:

'What time is it?'

He took out the gold hunter, opened it and said:

'Almost half five.'

'How long will it take us?'

'It's half an hour from here to the shore, an hour to row out.'

They began walking down the lane. Not wanting to be alongside him, she slowed. Twice he eased his stride, allowing her to catch up. Each time she deliberately lessened her pace. When this happened for the third time he stopped to ask:

'Are you tired?'

'A bit,' she said, 'you walk on, I'll keep you in sight.'

The flecked eyes blinked and then stared impassively. What had she said? What was the expression in hunting, and war? In sight? On sight? Sighting? Meaningless without a gun. What could he possibly suspect when she herself did not know what she would or could do? An opportunity might or might not arise. If it did she must seize it as quickly as he had jumped on the rat. Yes. 'Watch and seize' . . . the Winters' motto.

As they passed the bog-hole where the cow had died, he thumbed. She nodded, forcing a smile. They went on through the magical bogland of Brackagh round Laban, past the small reeded lake, and on through a succession of small fields, keeping close to the ditches, crossing the county road well below the thirty-acre scrub of Clonoula avenue. From there on the land sloped downwards leading to the ravine which dropped two hundred feet to the small rivulet cutting its way towards the lower lough and islands.

Ward found a downpath leading to the floor of the ravine. It went sideways. She followed him in a silence so absolute they could hear each other breathing as they slid from tree to bush to rock, down and down again through greying light into the primal gloom of fern and stone, of moss and twisted thorn. Like this for ten thousand years or longer: oak, elm and birch. It was like entering a great green wooded cave and far below the sound of water running over brown stones.

Once he had to take her hand to help at a steep place. The sudden mix of horror and heartbreak was so overwhelming that her vision became blinded, her speech thickened, and she could not hear what he was asking and kept saying:

'It's all right, it's nothing.'

'You're sure?'

'I'm sure,' knowing that far from being 'nothing', everything, the entirety of her life, had altered to night-mare.

He stopped, watching, as she wiped at her face with the back of her hands, carefully avoiding the swollen part around her left eye. When she had regained some control, she saw that he was still looking at her closely with an expression which could almost have passed for concern. Feigning? Smile and smile and be a villain? What where those lines about killing the thing you love most? For him it was killing the thing he loved least. For gold, not me: gold. But then he might be smiling just a little at the mother of his child. It seemed to her now, looking at Ward, that no creature in the world could ever be more dangerous than the creature he was, than the creature she was, than the creature within her.

Once down, they set out along the bank of the rivulet through elongated birch and alder, twice fording it to make the walking easier. She followed, aware that the ravine was widening above, a sense of greenish-grey light coming down. They must be nearing the lake shore. She asked the time again:

'Almost half six.'

Then suddenly, from the greenness of the rivulet, the openness of water, the immense sky and islands beckoning through a low mist. Like birth she thought . . . or death?

The tarred curragh was keeled up on a natural pier jutting into the water from the gravel shore. Ward righted it, pulled it to the water and held it steady while she stepped in. He then got in himself, pushed the boat away from the shore punt-wise, sat and began rowing strongly, rhythmically towards Corvey Island. The water was so still she could hear the whispered swish of the prow between oar-splashes. It was three miles or more from the lake shore to the island. It would take him well over half an hour to get there. Every chance she could, she studied his face: closed, clenched, absorbed. Once when he looked back, she glanced down and saw a small wooden bung on the floor of the curragh. In the middle of the bung there was a rusted cup-hook. It had been inserted into the floor with a piece of cloth. Clearly the bung had shrunk. It should not be too difficult to remove. Her heart began to argue with her breathing in a rapid familiar way. Supposing . . . Yes, but she could bloody her fingers trying to pull it out. He would see what she was doing. No, that would not work. She stared away across the lake. By now they were quarter of the way out. Every now and then her eyes were drawn back to the bung. It was when she saw the gaff, prised into the frame of the boat, that the battle between her heart and her lungs became so loud that she wondered if Ward could hear. For a minute or two she found it difficult to breathe. Gradually her heart settled. She glanced over at Ward. She saw him swallow and give a sallow smile. He said:

'Are you boat-sick?'

She pointed at her throat and muttered something in response. Soon they would be half-way there. Her whole body was on the edge of trembling. With an effort of will she controlled it. She began to think, decided, reached for the gaff, took it out, turned it over in her hands, looking at it with pretended indifference till she heard Ward's voice saying:

'The priest . . . that's what they call that.'

She looked back at him and said:

'Yes, I remember.'

For five minutes or so she let the gaff dangle beside her leg. When she was certain he was not looking, she hooked it through the rusted cup-hook on the bung. The priest. The end, no absolution. She let it lie thus on the floor of the Curragh for another five minutes. What next? If the bung came out easily, the bottom of the boat would fill slowly. Would he suspect, and then discover? Would he try to kill her? To what purpose?' No, she could get out and swim away. He couldn't follow in a water-logged cot. I'm being stupid, she thought. All I have to do is to take out this bung and cover it with my foot; the boat will fill, he'll panic and start to row. Long before the island she would tip the boat, push it away and he would have nothing to cling on to. He'd go down like a stone. What could be simpler? She would have to time it carefully because the water was cold for a long swim. But swimming itself should take care of that, and if she got tired she could float most of the way.

They were a little over half-way towards Corvey Island. She would have to decide now. Yes, *now*, a voice said. Do it now . . . now. She began to unlace the buttons of her boots and pull them off one by one. He glanced at what she was doing, indifferent. She heard herself say, 'these boots are new and tight.' He did not reply. She placed the boots where they would block the view of the bung. She then took off the jacket of her costume. He was still in no way alerted. Her skirt would slip off easily once in the water. She dangled the gaff, linking it into the cup-hook of the bung. Ward had begun to whistle.

She watched his mouth move as it shaped notes, an American melody she could not place. Should she jerk or turn? She began to turn slowly with both hands exerting an upward pull. Yes, she could sense the bung turn and there! – a sudden uprush of water, the coldness spilling about her feet. She placed one foot over the bung-hole to stop the flow, put the gaff back in the side of the curragh and stared out across the lake. It was a full three minutes before Ward noticed. His feet were up on the frame, well above the rising water. She had heard him mutter:

'Heavy old brute this.'

'I think', she said, 'we must have a leak somewhere.'

Ward stopped rowing, stared down at the water on the floor of the cot and said:

'Jesus! You're right.'

She nodded up towards his end.

'It's from behind you somewhere.'

As he twisted round he said:

'I can't swim.'

'Keep rowing,' she said, 'we're over half-way.'

He began to row strenuously. As he did she took her foot off the bung-hole. The water was now so deep on the floor that the swirl as it came up could not be detected. She could see the veins standing out on his neck and forehead. The boat had become dead-weight, almost static. When she leaned to one side it almost shipped water and he gave a hoarse cry:

'Quit! Take care; you'll cope us!'

There was such naked terror in his face that she looked away unable to say what she thought. She might say:

'I saw where you were digging with Blinky, now it's your turn to make your peace with God, to put on bravery.' Instead all she could say was:

'May God forgive you, my love, and me.'

There was nothing in his face but incomprehension and terror. As she shifted from the centre of the stern seat to the side, the curragh slipped over as easily as a toy boat. The water was bracing, so wintry-cold she scarcely heard the gurgling scream. She surfaced, arched her back, placed her feet on the stern and pushed the craft with all her strength. It moved away easily, more quickly than she had imagined. She followed, pushing it ahead of her, swimming away from the threshing and screeching in the water a few yards away, away from the horror of her name being screamed out again and again . . . 'Beth! Beth! Beth!' She was well away when she stopped pushing the curragh, turned on her back and floated, covering her ears tightly with her hands and kicking with her feet, both as a ploy to kill off the sound of Ward's drowning voice and to lessen the seizure of grief and horror which possessed her, body and soul.

How long does it take to drown a man? Unwanted pups and kittens, about three minutes. *That* she knew, and this thing of surfacing for the third, fourth or fifth time? True or false? Could she count up to a hundred? She began, and through the counting she could hear his voice . . . 'Beth! Beth!' . . . Aloud she began very slowly:

'I believe in God the Father Almighty, Creator of Heaven and Earth and in Jesus Christ His only Son

Our Lord . . . our only son . . . our only child . . . died and was buried . . . he tumbled down to hell . . . with the poor crooked . . . the third day he rose . . . by any other name . . . 'Beth! Beth! Beth!' . . . Oh sweet Jesus, he's still howling . . . how long . . . the third time he rose again from the dead . . . is that it? Is he gone now? He ascended into heaven and sitteth at the right hand of the Father . . . it's my left hand is smashed . . . and where's my father all my life? Where's he now? The Emperor of Russia was my father . . . Oh that he were alive now and here to see the flatness of my misery with eyes of pity . . . not revenge . . . oh no, sweet Jesus, no: it's not sweet . . . it's bitter and horrible. Silence . . . sinking, sinking, sinking to eternity, to hell? . . . Is he? Gone?

She opened her eyes, rolled over from floating to swimming and looked about. The mist had cleared. Silence. Nothing to see but swallows skimming over the calm surface of the lake. Above, a vast empty sky. After a while she saw the black shape of the capsized curragh, now a hundred yards away. It was too awful to contemplate or comprehend. She said to herself:

'My true love, my false love: gone. Farewell forever and forever and forever and forever, farewell.'

Gulping in water, choking with grief, she turned on her back again, floating, and said:

'Don't girn, idiot, swim or you'll join him.' She began to swim.

Aware of her skirt and shift dragging she wriggled out of them and set out with a steady breast-stroke towards Corvey Island, now quarter of a mile away. Between floating and swimming it took her the most of an hour to reach the island. The sun was high and warm as she walked ashore. For ten minutes she rested in the grassy hollow of the garden, then made her way up to the bothy, found the key, unlocked the door and set about lighting a fire.

The matches were so damp that she had to strike most of a box before one ignited. When the kindling began to blaze, she wrung out vest and knickers, hung them on a chair near the fire, opened the settle bed, wrapped herself in blankets and closed her throbbing eyes. She found herself at the bottom of a river or lake, in a dark cavern. All round her were infants crying soundlessly and floating past, warriors staring bitterly with gaping wounds, old men and women grief-hobbled, and the red dwarf with a wattle creel on his back, gold spilling out of it. He was pointing and laughing. She realised she was herself underwater. Terrified of drowning she began to swim upwards towards the light and broke the surface with a great cry as her lungs gulped in air. She swam ashore. Someone was calling her name, a familiar voice. She realised it was Liam, her love. She pointed across a small bay at rowanberries on the other bank and said, 'Those berries, be sure to bring me some,' and he swam back and brought a branch of the berries in his mouth and it seemed to her now that nothing in the world could be more beautiful than to be watching him cross the dark pool, his white body perfect and his black hair and the green of his gold-flecked eyes, a youth without fault or blemish, the branch of red rowanberries between his throat and shapely face. When he got out of the water she could not see him, only feel him, and then realised it was the top of his head. He seemed asleep. She sat up and grasped his buttocks, astonished at the ease with which his head slipped into her body, without forcing, without effort. When he began to struggle she crossed her ankles, tightening. Relief was slow in coming. Part of her mind wondered a little about his breathing, another part said: 'Good enough for the murderous brute.'

Pleasured, she pushed him away with violent disgust, and saw with even deeper disgust the swollen tongue lolling in his mouth, his eyes upturned, and heard herself say: 'He's dead, fish-dead, my love has eyes like Parnell, and he's fish-dead,' and again she heard a familiar voice calling her name. She could see now, through the open bothy door, the evening light on the lough.

Then she saw the familiar figure of Billy Winters, running towards the open door. He stood, arms outstretched, leaning inwards, blocking the light.

When his eyes became accustomed to the half-light, Billy Winters saw Beth on the settle bed half elbowed-up and staring towards the door with one desolate and one dark-rimmed eye. Gradually, as she began to make out his features, it occurred to her that the same face which had manifested such hatred and incomprehension twelve hours ago now seemed haunted, taut with guilt and concern.

Then he was kneeling beside her, holding her and kissing her hands and forehead, moving from her awful bruised face and back to her swollen left hand, all the while sobbing as she had once heard him sob at her mother's grave. Twice he tried to speak. Each time he was so overcome he could not utter. He kept shaking his head until finally he said:

'I was certain you were gone; I saw one of your boots below in the shallows near Ward and I thought, she's gone; she's dead, the light of my life, I've driven out, I've killed the only thing . . . I . . . I've . . .' and again he was overcome. She watched him till control returned. He got off his knees, took over a stool and sat by her. As she pulled the blankets about her neck like a bib he said:

'There's a bad twist in you, girl, do you know that?'

'I do . . . but there's worse in you, Sir, and you don't know it.'

Silence.

'How did you guess I was here?'

'The Dummy McGonnell . . . Did they harm you, girl?'

'Nothing visible; you did that.'

'A terrible mistake . . . but you were robbing me, girl, for him, for Ward, for your *lover* . . . could you not guess what he was? Murderous, evil brute.'

'And what are you, Sir . . . or any man . . . I loved him.' Suddenly overwhelmed, she averted her face and began crying into her hands. When she stopped she could hear his voice as though far away under water or through glass, as in a dream, and it was saying:

'The lowest of the low. Could you not guess?'

'I loved him; surely *you* can understand that, can you not?'

For a long time neither said anything. She did not venture to speak. Eventually he asked: 'How did he drown?'

'Loudly . . . squalidly. I think his bowels must have opened.'

'Yes; but how?'

'He can't swim; I pulled the bung; the curragh filled with water and went down, and he with it . . .'

Billy Winters thought about this.

'A drowning accident, "death by misadventure", that's what they'll call it.'

'I don't care what they call it.'

'Nor do I but I care deeply about you, daughter.'

'I'm not your daughter.'

'Can you forgive me ever, Beth?'

'Not today, nor tomorrow, not ever, maybe.'

'The broken tree forgives the storm.'

'And stays broken.'

'It can grow again: I'd care for you different from this day out.'

'I hate you, Billy Winters, and if I'd courage enough I'd kill you too, and feel nothing.'

She saw him glance at her. He was shaking his head: 'You wouldn't.'

'I would; for what you did to Mama, to me, to God knows who else. I will always hate you.'

'I will always love you, Beth Winters.'

When Beth did not respond he moved towards the bothy door to look out on the heart-breaking loveliness, the seeming peace of a May evening. He became aware then of the island shore-line and the amber darkness where Ward lay in the shallows – or was he floating now in a deep current down the lough towards the mother of all, staring up at the stars through a haemorrhage of dying light? A raven gliding over from Tirkennedy circled the sunken garden three times before alighting near the well. From cupped hands they had drunk there on that other May day long ago, one calendar month before God withheld his mercy to allow the slaughter of his wife and unborn child.

For about a minute neither spoke. Then he said:

'We're a pair, we two: cangled both to treachery. Maybe we should marry, go elsewhere?'

Beth put her hands under the blankets onto her womb, and lay back, turning her face to the wall. When he saw this he asked:

'Are you hurting . . . are you sick, Beth?'

'Unto death, Mr Winters . . . unto death.'

A SELECTED LIST OF CONTEMPORARY FICTION
AVAILABLE IN VINTAGE

☐	GIRLS HIGH	Barbara Anderson	£5.99
☐	FALL ON YOUR KNEES	Ann-Marie MacDonald	£6.99
☐	I WAS AMELIA EARHART	Jane Mendelsohn	£5.99
☐	BIRDSONG	Sebastian Faulks	£6.99
☐	THE EBONY TOWER	John Fowles	£6.99
☐	THE MAGUS	John Fowles	£7.99
☐	THE FOLDING STAR	Alan Hollinghurst	£6.99
☐	THE PRINCE OF WEST END AVENUE	Alan Isler	£5.99
☐	THE CONVERSATIONS AT CURLOW CREEK	David Malouf	£5.99
☐	REMEMBERING BABYLON	David Malouf	£6.99
☐	THE GIANT'S HOUSE	Elizabeth McCracken	£5.99
☐	ENDURING LOVE	Ian McEwan	£5.99
☐	BELOVED	Toni Morrison	£6.99
☐	TAR BABY	Toni Morrison	£6.99
☐	SELECTED STORIES	Alice Munro	£6.99
☐	THE WAY I FOUND HER	Rose Tremain	£6.99
☐	LADDER OF YEARS	Anne Tyler	£5.99

- All Vintage books are available through mail order or from your local bookshop.

- Please send cheque/eurocheque/postal order (sterling only), Access, Visa, Mastercard, Diners Card, Switch or Amex:

☐☐☐☐☐☐☐☐☐☐☐☐☐☐☐☐

Expiry Date:_____ Signature:_____

Please allow 75 pence per book for post and packing U.K.
Overseas customers please allow £1.00 per copy for post and packing.

ALL ORDERS TO:
Vintage Books, Books by Post, TBS Limited, The Book Service, Colchester Road, Frating Green, Colchester, Essex CO7 7DW

NAME:_____

ADDRESS:_____

_____

_____

Please allow 28 days for delivery. Please tick box if you do not wish to receive any additional information ☐

Prices and availability subject to change without notice.